18TH RACE

ISSUE IN DOUBT

— BOOK: 1 —

18TH RACE

ISSUE IN DOUBT

—— BOOK: 1 ——

DAVID SHERMAN

eBooks
Stratford, NJ

PUBLISHED BY
eSpec Books LLC
Danielle McPhail, Publisher
PO Box 493,
Stratford, New Jersey 08084
www.especbooks.com

Previously published by DTF Publications, an imprint of Dark Quest Books, 2013

ISBN: 978-1-942990-42-0
ISBN (eBook): 978-1-942990-43-7

Copyediting: Keith R.A. DeCandido
Design: Mike and Danielle McPhail
Cover Art: Mike McPhail, McP Digital Graphics
www.mikemcphail.com
www.milscifi.com

This book is dedicated to the memory of:

Corporal John F. Mackie

The first US Marine to earn
The Medal of Honor;
At the Battle of Drewry's Bluff
May 15, 1862

PROLOG: FIRST CONTACT

McKinzie Elevator Base, Outside Millerton,
Semi-Autonomous World Troy

SAMUEL ROGERS JERKED WHEN HE HEARD THE BEEPING OF THE PROXIMITY alert. He spun in his chair to look at the approach displays and his jaw dropped. With one hand he toggled the space-comm to hail the incoming ship, with the other he reached for the local comm to call Frederick Franklin, his boss.

Franklin sounded groggy when he answered. "This better be good, Rogers. I just got to sleep."

"Sorry, Chief, but are we expecting any starships? One just popped up half an AU north. Uh oh."

"No, we aren't expecting anyone. And what do you mean, 'uh oh'?"

"Chief—" Rodgers' voice broke and he had to start again. "Chief, data coming in says the incoming starship is three klicks wide."

"Bullshit," Franklin snapped. "There aren't any starships that big!"

"I know. It's got to be an asteroid. And it's on an intercept vector."

"There aren't any asteroids north." Franklin's voice dropped to a barely intelligible mumble. "North, that would explain how it 'just popped up.'" Indistinct noises sounded to Rogers like his boss was getting dressed. "Have you tried to hail her?"

"The same time I called you. But half an AU..."

"Yeah, yeah, I know. Stand by, I'm on my way."

"Standing by." Rogers sounded relieved.

Franklin burst into the spaceport's operations room and headed straight for the approach displays. In seconds he absorbed the data, and let out a grunt.

"Any reply yet?" he asked.

Rogers shook his head. "Too soon, Chief."

Franklin grimaced; he should have realized that and not have asked such a dumb question. The starship—asteroid, whatever—was half an Astronomical Unit out, half the distance from old Earth to Sol. It would take about four minutes for the hail to reach the incoming object, and another four minutes for a reply to come back. Plus however much time it would take for whoever it was to decide to answer the hail. The two men watched the data display as time ticked by.

After watching for another fifteen minutes, with no reply, and nothing but confirmation as to its velocity, vector, and probable impact time, Franklin decided to kick the problem upstairs.

"Office of the President." James Merton's voice was thick when he answered the president's comm; the night duty officer must have been dozing.

"Jim, Fred here. We've got a situation that requires some attention from the boss."

"Can it wait until morning? Bill's had a long day, and he's dead to the world."

"Come morning, it might be too late to do anything."

"Come on, Fred," Merton said. "No offense intended, but you're an elevator operator. What kind of earth-shattering problem can you possibly have?"

"Exactly that: a literally earth-shattering problem. There's a large object on an intercept course. That's large, as in planet-buster. It'll be here in less than a standard day."

There was a momentary silence before Merton asked, "You aren't kidding, are you?"

"I wish. Stand by for the data." Franklin nodded to Rogers, who transmitted a data set to the president's office. A minute later, Franklin and Rogers heard Merton swear under his breath.

"You called it, something that big really is a planet buster, isn't it?" the duty officer asked.

"Unfortunately," Franklin answered.

"Now, according to the data you sent me, the object is metallic, and it seems to have the density of a starship rather than the density of an asteroid. Am I reading those figures right?"

"You're reading right ," Franklin said. "But nobody makes starships that big."

"At least nobody we know of," Rogers murmured. "Have you tried to contact it, I mean, in case it *is* a starship?"

"Yes, we did." Franklin looked at Rogers, who held up four fingers. "Four times. No response."

"And you're sure it's on a collision course?"

Franklin shivered. "Absolutely."

"Keep trying to make contact. I'll wake the president."

An hour and a half later, a three-man Navy rescue team under the command of Lieutenant (j.g.) Cyrus Hayden, rode the elevator up to Base 1, in geosynchronous orbit, where they boarded the tender *John Andrews* to take a closer look at the rapidly approaching object. If it was a starship their orders were to again attempt radio contact. If she did not reply, to attempt to board her. If the object was an unusual asteroid, Hayden and his men were to plant a nuclear device on its side, then back off to a safe distance before detonating the bomb. It was hoped that the explosion would deflect the object's course enough to avoid the collision that was looking more certain with each passing minute.

The North American Union Navy tender *John Andrews* was still 100,000 kilometers from the object when laser beams lanced out from it and shredded the tender.

Twenty shocked minutes later, the orbital lasers of Troy's defensive batteries shot beams of coherent light. The only effect the lasers seemed to have on the object, which was now obviously a warship from some unknown people, was to provide the enemy with the location of the defensive weapons. Within minutes, all of Troy's orbital laser batteries were knocked out by counter-battery fire from the enemy starship. It had committed an act of war when it vaporized the *John Andrews*, hadn't it? Didn't that make it the enemy?

When the enemy starship was a quarter million kilometers out, it fired braking rockets, which slowed its speed and altered its vector enough to reach high orbit rather than colliding with the planet. Small objects began flicking off it and heading toward the surface.

Ground-based laser and missile batteries began firing at the small vessels. The mother-ship killed those batteries as easily as she had killed the orbital batteries.

Shortly after that the first landers made planetfall, and reports of wholesale slaughter began coming in, William F. Lukes, President of Troy, ordered all the data they had on the invasion uploaded onto drones and the drones launched: Destination Earth.

The unidentified enemy killed the first several drones, but stopped shooting them when it became obvious that they were running away rather than attacking.

Two days later, four of the drones reached the Sol System via wormhole. It took ten more days for a North American Union Navy frigate to pick one of them up and carry it to Garroway Base on Mars, from where its coded message was transmitted to the NAU's Supreme Military Headquarters on Earth.

MAJOR GENERAL JOSEPH H. DE CASTRO SWEPT PAST THE GUARDS STANDING outside the entrance to the offices of the Chairman of the Joint Chiefs of Staff and marched through the cavernous, darkly paneled outer office directly to the desk of Colonel Nicholas Fox, which sat below the colors of all the military services of the NAU.

"Nick," de Castro said, "I need to see the Chairman, right now. I don't care who he's meeting with."

Fox leaned back in his chair and looked up at de Castro with mild curiosity. "Joe, you know I can't let people just barge in on the Chairman." He shook his head. "His schedule today is packed tighter than a constipated jarhead. Maybe if he stops by the Flag Club later on, you can get a minute or two with him. Can't help you, Joe." Fox then looked intently at his console, as though he had pressing business to attend to. His behavior was insubordinate, but in this office, acting in his official capacity as gatekeeper to the Chairman, he effectively outranked anybody with fewer than four stars, and de Castro had only two.

"If you knew what I have here," de Castro tapped the right breast pocket of his uniform jacket, "you wouldn't be wasting my time. I'd already be telling the Chairman what I've got."

"So tell me what you've got. I'll decide if it's important enough to disrupt the Chairman's schedule."

De Castro glowered at Fox for a few seconds, then said, steely-voiced, "Have it your way, Nick. You can explain to the Chairman why I had to jump the chain." He about-faced to march out, but Fox stopped him before he'd taken more than two steps.

"Wait a minute, Joe. What do you mean, 'jump the chain'?"

De Castro half turned back. "I'm going fifty paces. This can't wait." Fifty paces was the distance from where he was to the offices of the Secretary of War.

"You wouldn't!" Fox said, shocked.

"I will."

Colonel Fox opened his mouth to say something more, but thought for a couple of seconds before he spoke. "Wait one," he said, and tapped his desk comm, the direct line to the Chairman's inner sanctum.

"Sir," he said apologetically when the Chairman came on, "Major General de Castro is here. He says he has something that requires the Secretary's immediate attention." He paused to listen, answered, "No sir, he won't tell me what it is." Another pause to listen. "I'll tell him, sir." He looked at de Castro. "He'll see you in a minute or so."

De Castro faced the door leading deeper into the Chairman's offices, and stood at ease, patiently waiting. A moment later, the door opened and de Castro snapped to attention. Fleet Admiral Ira Clinton Welborn, Chairman of the Joint Chiefs of Staff, ushered out a man de Castro recognized as Field Marshal Carl Ludwig, Welborn's counterpart in the European Union's military. Welborn was making placating noises, and assuring Ludwig that he would have dinner with him at the Flag Club that evening.

As soon as the EU's military chief was gone, Welborn turned on de Castro and snarled. "This better be good. I've been getting close to a diplomatic breakthrough with that martinet, and you might have just bollixed it!"

"It is, sir," de Castro said in a strong voice.

"Follow." Welborn headed back to his inner sanctum. De Castro followed a pace behind and slightly to Welborn's left. The two marched along a darkly wainscoted corridor with offices branching off to both sides, toward a wider space at the end, where a navy petty officer sat at a desk working on a comp. Two Marines in dress blues, a first lieutenant and a gunnery sergeant, both armed with holstered sidearms, stood at parade rest flanking the doorway to the inner sanctum. The two came to attention at Welborn's approach. De Castro couldn't help but notice that the gunnery sergeant had several more rows of ribbons on his chest than he himself did, and the lieutenant had nearly as many as the gunny. It was obvious that the Marines were from the combat arms.

"Siddown," Welborn snapped as the petty officer began to stand. She did and returned to her work. "Close it," he snarled at the Marines. The door to the inner sanctum closed silently behind de Castro when the two swept past.

Inside was an office only slightly less opulent than that of the Secretary of War himself. Its walls were covered with pictures of warships: paintings, engravings, lithographs, photographs, and holograms. Wooden ships: with rams and oars; with sails; with sails and cannon; iron clad with sails; iron clad with sails and steam engines. Steel ships: with guns in turrets, aircraft carriers with and without turrets and missiles. Space-going warships.

Welborn headed for his massive desk and dropped into the leather-upholstered executive chair behind it. "All right, de Castro, what do you have?" He didn't offer a seat.

"This came in ten minutes ago, sir," de Castro said as he fingered a crystal out of his right breast pocket. "By your leave, sir?" He made to insert the crystal in the comp to the side of the desk. Welborn grunted assent, and de Castro completed the action. In a second, a report appeared on the console. Welborn quickly read through it.

"Images?"

"They're garbled, sir. The cryptographer who decoded the message and the watch officer who delivered it from her to me are attempting to clean them up now."

"Is anybody helping them?"

"Only if they're disobeying my orders. I instructed them to keep this between themselves, and to discuss it with nobody but me."

"Good. Instruct your security personnel to quarantine them as soon as they're done. And I want the images zipped to me the instant they're intelligible, no matter where I am. Right now, you and I are going to see the Secretary."

De Castro called in the orders to isolate the cryptographer and the watch officer as he followed the Chairman out of the office. He didn't even glance at Colonel Fox as he passed through the outer office. Four minutes later, the two were face to face with Richmond P. Hobson, the Secretary of War himself, one of the three most important and powerful people in the entire North American Union.

Hobson seated them in a conversational group of chairs around a small table, and made small talk while a Navy steward poured coffee. De Castro, who had never before been in this office, glanced around. Portraits were hung above dark blond wainscoting that looked like it might be real oak. De Castro recognized enough of the faces in the paintings to know that they were previous NAU Secretaries of War, and the Secretaries of Defense of the old United States, the Canadian Ministers of Defence, and the Mexican Ministers of Defense going back to the beginning of the twentieth century free-trade agreement among the three countries—the precursor of the North American Union.

Hobson took a sip of coffee as the steward exited, then asked, "Well, Ira, what does J2 have that's so important that you have to bring its director to me on such short notice?"

"Show him," Welborn said.

"Yes sir." De Castro looked around for a comp. Hobson pressed a button on the side of his chair and one arose from the side of the coffee table. "Thank you, sir." De Castro inserted the crystal. He angled the display so the Secretary could read the report without leaning to the side.

After a moment, Hobson sat back. "How firm is this?"

"We haven't had time to verify, sir," de Castro said. "This only came in about fifteen minutes ago."

"What about images?"

Welborn told him that the garbled images were being worked on, but he expected to have something shortly. De Castro nodded agreement.

"We have to tell the President instantly," Hobson said. "And get State in on it." He pressed another button on the side of his chair, and a Navy lieutenant commander appeared inside the door.

"Tom," Hobson addressed him, "kindly contact your counterparts at the President's office and SecState, and inform them that I request a meeting at the earliest possible moment. Emphasize that it's of the gravest importance."

"Aye aye, sir." The lieutenant commander about-faced and exited.

"Tom Irving," Hobson told Welborn and de Castro, "good man." He looked directly at Welborn. "When his tour with me is over, he deserves to have three full stripes, and be given a command."

Welborn nodded. "Sir, with a recommendation like that, I think a promotion and command assignment will be expedited."

"Do you think we should send a reconnaissance mission to Troy?" Hobson asked Welborn, getting back to the topic at hand.

"Yes, sir, I do."

"I hoped you'd say that. Who do you recommend?"

"Marine Force Recon."

"Oh?" Hobson cocked his head. "Not SEALs or Rangers?"

"No, sir. Force Recon. While both SEALs and Rangers are adept at intelligence gathering, they spend as much time training in commando strikes. Force Recon spends almost all of its time and energy 'snooping and pooping,' as they call it, gathering intelligence. They fight only *in extremis*, and believe their mission has failed if they have to fight. I don't want anybody fighting until we know who—or what—we're up against."

"Very good. How soon can Force Recon deploy a sufficient number of teams?"

"Within three days after an operation order is drawn up, sir. Possibly sooner. *Probably* sooner."

"Very good. Get started on the op order as soon as you can. I'll authorize deploying the Marines as soon as the President gives his permission."

"Aye aye, sir," the Chairman said.

De Castro jerked; his comm had vibrated. He looked at it. "Excuse me, sirs, I think I should take this."

Hobson gestured for him to rise and take the call. De Castro stepped away a few feet before answering his comm. He listened for a moment, said something, listened again, gave an order, broke the connection, and resumed his seat.

"Sirs, three more drones from Troy have been brought in. They all have the same message as the one you've seen. One of them had a few usable images. They are being sent to all three of us."

"Good!" Hobson rubbed his hands briskly and looked at the comp. In seconds, it signaled incoming traffic from J2. "I'll put them up on the big screen." He pressed another button on his chair, and a two-by-three-meter display screen rose on the wall behind the grouping where they sat. After a few touches on his comp controls, a slide show began on the display.

The three men watched in stunned silence as little more than half a dozen images, some stills and some vids, rotated through. None of the pictures were fully in focus, and some had scrambled—or completely missing—portions. But they all showed the attackers, and the slaughter they wrought.

The third time through, Hobson cleared his throat and said softly, "We always suspected they were still out there." He pressed the button that summoned his aide.

"Tom, have you heard back from the President or State yet?" he asked.

"Sir," Irving said, "they're coordinating a time, and will let us know instantly."

Hobson stood, Welborn and de Castro jumped to their feet as well.

"Instantly isn't fast enough. Get my car, and tell the President's office and State that we're on our way to the Prairie Palace."

"Aren't you meeting with Marshal Ludwig today?" Hobson asked Welborn as the three headed for the Secretary's vehicle.

"Yes, sir. I broke off my meeting with him to bring this to you. I'm having dinner with him at the Flag Club later."

"Whatever you do, unless the President orders otherwise, *don't* let him know about this until I tell you to."

"Ludwig's sharp, sir. He'll know there's something important I'm not telling him." Welborn flexed his shoulders. "But I'm sharp, too. I'll manage to avoid offending him."

The Prairie Palace, Omaha,
Douglas County, Federal Zone, NAU

When the United States of America, Canada, and Mexico merged into the NAU, none of the three would accept either of the other's national capital for the capital of the new Union. They settled on Omaha, Nebraska because it was situated roughly in the middle of the continent. Moreover, Omaha was cold enough in the winter to satisfy Canadians' yen for the Great White North, and hot enough in the summer for the Mexicans to fondly remember the deserts of

Sonora and Chihuahua—or so it was said. As for the USA, Omaha was a major part of the Great American Heartland, being an established city of the second tier. It and Douglas County were fully adequate for a capital city. Sarpy County, directly to the south, was the home of Offutt Air Force Base, one-time headquarters of the Strategic Air Command, an ideal location for the new Supreme Military Headquarters. And Pottawatomie County, Iowa, directly across the Missouri River from Omaha, provided more than ample space for the buildings needed to house what was sure to be a massive central bureaucracy. Some in Nebraska strenuously objected to losing Douglas and Sarpy, and Iowa to losing Pottawatomie to the new Federal Zone. They were reminded of the benefits previously enjoyed by the parts of Maryland and Virginia adjacent to the District of Columbia—not to mention the additional taxes garnered by those states from the increased population of government workers who lived in adjacent counties—and graciously agreed to losing those population centers.

Competitions were held to design the new Union's legislative capitol and the presidential residence and office. Nobody other than the bureaucrats who selected it was happy with the monumental faux sod-house design of the president's residence and office, christened "The Prairie Palace," although nearly everybody outside government came to agree that it was appropriate that the legislative Capitol was erected on what had once been the stock yards for the South Omaha slaughter houses.

It was to the Prairie Palace, located on the site of what had once been Central High School, that Secretary Hobson, Chairman Welborn, and Deputy Director de Castro went to see the President of the NAU.

The Round Office, The Prairie Palace

Albert Leopold Mills, tall and lean, in his late fifties, was a distinguished, mild-mannered gentleman. Until he got behind closed doors.

"What the fuck is the meaning of this!" he demanded as soon as the door to the Round Office closed behind his visitors from military headquarters. "I have more important things to do than sit around in a circle jerk with you. I should have all of your resignations on my desk within the hour!"

"Sir, if you don't agree that what's on this," Hobson held up a crystal, "is worth disrupting your schedule, you'll have my resignation as soon as I can scribble it out."

"We'll see about that." Mills snatched the crystal from Hobson's fingers. He popped it into his comp and scanned the text report. Then reread it more slowly. "Who did it?"

"Sir, we don't know for certain who they are, but there are images," Hobson said.

"Show me."

Hobson nodded to de Castro, who stepped to the President's desk and took control of the console to show the images.

"They aren't all of the best quality, sir," de Castro said as he activated the first image. It was an eleven-second vid, bouncy as though the person shooting it was trembling and had forgotten to stabilize the view. It showed armed—*creatures*—racing along a street. Heavily muscled legs ending in taloned feet propelled them faster than a human could run, even a human augmented with military armor. They were bent at the hips, their torsos held parallel to the ground. Sinuous necks, triple the length of a human's, held their heads up, and whipped them side to side. The faces jutted forward, with long jaws that seemed to be filled with sharp, conical teeth. Arms little more than half the length of their legs held weapons that could have been some kind of rifle. A crest of feathery structures ran from the tops of their faces all the way down their spines, where fans of long, feathery structures jutted backward providing a counterbalance to their forward-thrusting torsos. Their knees bent backward, like birds'. They appeared to be naked except for straps and pouches arrayed around their bodies. Packs of smaller creatures that might have been juveniles of their kind sped among them.

Mills was expressionless looking at the vid to the end. "Next."

De Castro activated the second image. This one was a grainy still shot, showing one of the creatures rising up slightly from horizontal to put its rifle-like weapon to its shoulder.

The third image was another vid, seventeen seconds long this time. It had been garbled along the way, and parts of the image were so badly pixilated they couldn't be made out. But it showed enough to make clear what was happening. Packs of the smaller creatures were leaping onto people, shredding them with their talons, ripping into them with their toothy jaws.

Two more stills showed one of the creatures biting chunks out of a downed woman.

A thirty-three-second vid, taken from behind defensive works from which the human soldiers of the battalion assigned to Troy's defense were fighting, showed the creatures and their packs of small companions assaulting the position. They ran zigging and zagging randomly, almost too fast for the eye to follow. Some of the creatures were hit, and tumbled to the ground, presumably dead or severely wounded. But those hits were by chance; the creatures moved too fast to be hit by aimed fire. The last few seconds of the vid showed the creatures and their packs bounding over the defensive works to land among the soldiers and begin ripping them apart.

"That's enough," Mills said softly; he could see that there was another image or two that hadn't been run. He took a moment to compose himself, then said to Hobson, "You were right to bring this to my attention immediately. It was worth disrupting my schedule." He tapped his inter-office comm. "Where's State?" he barked into it.

"She's entering the building now, sir," came the reply.

"Well, get her tail in here instantly!"

Mills turned to Welborn. "What's our first step?"

"Sir, I've already given orders to draw up an operation order for a Force Recon platoon to head for Troy and get usable intelligence on the situation."

"How soon will it be ready?"

"By morning."

"And how soon after that can the Marines go?"

"As soon as you give authorization, sir."

"You've got it. I want to know what's happened out there."

There was a discrete knock and the door of the Round Office eased open.

"About time you got here, Walker," Mills snapped.

Mary E. Walker, NAU Secretary of State, stopped flat-footed and glared at the President. "Sir, I was in the middle of delicate negotiations with the EU Foreign Minister when I received Richmond's message. He failed to say what was so grave about the matter. I couldn't walk out without an explanation. As it is, when I told him about your summons, he gave the distinct impression that by the time I get back, he might be on his way back to Luxembourg."

"Then good riddance! We just got word of something much more important than the feelings of an overly sensitive Euro. Take a look." He angled his comp's display toward her and activated the image of the vid showing the assault on the defense battalion.

"What?" the Secretary of State gasped when the vid had run its course. "Where?" She looked distinctly green.

"Troy," Hobson said softly. "This came in..." He looked at de Castro.

"About forty-five minutes ago, ma'am," the J2 director said.

"Is it *them*?" she asked. "The ruins?"

The President looked at the other men for an answer to the question he'd wondered himself.

Welborn replied, "We have no way of knowing. But, yeah, I imagine so. Or if not whoever it was that destroyed those other civilizations, then somebody maybe just as bad." In its spread through space, humanity had discovered ruins left by seventeen non-human civilizations. One of them was on the level of the pyramid builders of ancient Earth, while most of them had technologically developed far enough to be on the threshold of interstellar travel—one actually seemed to have achieved it.

"They had no word? No ultimatum? No warning?" Walker asked.

"Not that we know of, ma'am," de Castro said when the President looked at him. "We have a text message saying they were under attack by an unknown enemy, and a few images. You just saw one of them; it isn't necessarily the worst."

"We need to alert everybody," Walker said. "If you'll excuse me, sir, I'll notify Minister Neahr right now." She turned away, reaching for her comm.

"You'll do no such thing!" Mills snapped.

"Sir?" She spun back to him, shocked by both his tone and the words.

"Until we know exactly what's happening on Troy, this is strictly need-to-know—and Zachariah C. Neahr doesn't need to know."

"But—"

"No buts," Mills cut her off. "I'd rather present all the worlds that humanity is on with a *fait accompli* than unnecessarily cause a panic.

Your job in this, Madam Secretary, is to keep the rest of the world in the dark about NAU's upcoming offworld troop movements."

"You're going to send our soldiers into, into *that*?" she asked, appalled.

Mills curled his lip at her. "As you would know if you hadn't been so tardy getting here, we're sending Force Recon to gather intelligence. Then we'll send a counter-invasion force in to clear out those...those *creatures*." He turned to Hobson and Welborn. "I want you to stand up a counter-invasion force, and ready Navy shipping to get them there once we know what we're up against."

"Right away, sir," Hobson said.

"Aye aye, sir." Welborn grinned. What was the point of having a Navy that traveled the stars, and command of one of the largest and most powerful militaries in all of human history if he never got to give the orders to attack an entire world?

"I'll notify Congress once the counter-invasion force is on its way," Mills said. "Now get everything moving."

De Castro didn't say anything, but he wondered how the President was going to justify taking military action without an Act of Congress authorizing it, or without even consulting with the Congressional leadership.

Launch Bay, NAUS Monticello,
in Semi-Autonomous World Troy space

FIRST LIEUTENANT MITCHELL PAIGE GAVE THE TWENTY MARINES OF HIS SECTION a final look over—he'd already inspected them—before saying a few words prior to them entering their landing craft. His Marines weren't exactly invisible, but he'd have had a hard time picking them out in the dim light if they hadn't had their helmets and gloves off. The patterning of the utilities worn by Force Recon tricked the eye into looking *beyond* them instead of registering *on* them.

"Marines, we don't know what you're going to find on Troy." Paige ignored the quiet chuckles that statement brought from the Marines. "That's why Force Recon is going in, to find out."

Some of the Marines exchanged glances: *No shit Sherlock. That's what Force Recon does; we go in to find out when nobody knows dick.*

"The *Monticello* been listening on all frequencies since exiting the wormhole, but as of—" Paige checked his watch. "—three minutes ago, no transmissions have been picked up, nor has anything registered on any of the ship's sensors. So we know no more than we did when we left Earth." He gave a wolfish grin. "That's why the Union called on us. We're going to find out, and then some alien ass is going to get kicked!"

"OOH-RAH!" the twenty Marines roared. None of them said, or even thought, anything about the fact that their commander wasn't going planetside with them. Everyone understood an officer going along with a Force Recon squad on a mission would only be in the way.

"Mount up!" Paige bellowed over the cheers. The Force Recon Marines pulled on their helmets and gloves as they filed into the landing craft and the waiting Squad Pods. One Marine in each squad carried a rifle. The other Marines were armed only with sidearms and knives—purely defensive weapons.

Paige watched until the landing craft's ramp closed, then gruffly said, "Let's go," and ducked through the hatch from the launch bay. Gunnery Sergeant Robert H. McCard, the first section chief, followed. The two Marines headed for the Command and Communications Center, where Captain Jefferson J. DeBlanc, 2nd Force Recon Company's executive officer, and the company's First Sergeant John H. Leims waited for them. Along the way, they had to press against the side of the narrow passageway to let the platoon's second section pass on its way to the launch bay.

It wasn't long before the officers, senior non-commissioned officers, and communications men of 2nd Force Recon Company (B) were gathered in C&C, and eight Force Recon squads were on their way to the surface of Troy.

The *Cayuga* Class frigate *Monticello* was a stealth vessel, specially configured to support Marine Force Recon and small raiding parties. To that end, she had a compartment equipped with comm gear to allow a command element to communicate with its planetside elements via burst microwaves, and give it directions as needed. Her external shape had odd, unexpected angles designed to reflect radar signals in directions other than back at a radar receiver. A coating over the entire hull except for the exhausts was designed to absorb and/or deflect other detection methods. Strategically placed vanes and trailing stringers dispersed heat from the exhausts, giving the starship a faint, easily overlooked heat signature. She was not designed for offensive fighting; her weapons and counter-weapon systems were strictly defensive.

Two hours earlier, the *Monticello* had exited a wormhole two light minutes northeast of Troy and slowly drifted planetward while using all of her passive sensors to search for spacecraft loitering in the area of her destination world. The warship also constantly scanned the planet's surface for signs of life, human or alien. When no signs of any presence, human or alien, were detected either in space or on the surface, the order was given for the landing party to prepare to head planetside.

The *Monticello*'s equally stealthed landing craft were each capable of landing up to fifty fully armed infantrymen on the surface of a planet, or launching four "Squad Pods" into the upper atmosphere for scattered planetfall. They were called "Spirits," both because they were as visible to standard detection methods as ethereal spirits and because they could spirit troops to or away from a planet's surface. The Squad Pods were intended to be mistaken for meteorites during their transit through an atmosphere: an ablative coating was designed to stop burning as soon as the antigrav drive kicked in when the pod was close to the ground, giving the impression that the meteorite had burned up. The Squad Pods normally landed away from populated areas, and flew nape-of-the-earth to their final destinations.

The eight Force Recon squads landed on Troy at widely separated locations so they could cover as much territory as possible. Upon completion of their missions, the Marines would return to their Squad Pods and rendezvous with the landing craft for return to the *Monti-cello*, where she maintained station near the collapsed entrance to the wormhole.

The *Monticello* stood ready to reopen the wormhole on fifteen minutes notice, either to return to Earth with the Marines, or to flee from an approaching enemy starship.

Planetfall, Semi-Autonomous World Troy

Squad Pod Alpha-1, with First squad aboard, plunged to the ground near the McKinzie Elevator Base. Its meteorite-mimicking track blinked out two and a half kilometers above the surface when its antigrav engine cut in to bring the small craft down twenty-seven kilometers distant, gently enough to avoid injuring its passengers, then scooted along, barely above the ground, to its final destination. Squad Pod Alpha-4, carrying Fourth squad, made planetfall on the opposite side of Millerton from the elevator base. Pods Alpha-2 and 3, and Bravo-1, 2, and 3 made planetfall in other locations on East Shapland, the primary settled continent on Troy.

Squad Pod Bravo-4 was the only one to visit the continent called West Shapland, which only had one settlement; some twelve thousand souls resided in and around the coastal fishing town of Pikestown. There was less than two minutes from the time the first pod reached its landing zone until the final one touched down on its.

Foot of the McKinzie Elevator Base,
Millerton, Semi-Autonomous World Troy

Staff Sergeant Jack Lummus, leader of the First squad, didn't give any orders when his Marines dashed off Alpha-1; touchdown was a well-rehearsed maneuver, and everyone knew what to do. The five Marines darted off in five different directions and went to ground fifty meters away from the pod, facing away from it. Each Marine had his motion detector, air sniffer, and infrared receiver operating before he took cover in one of the many craters that pocked the tarmac. Lummus didn't even say anything when his four men all reported they were in position and searching. Not that he was concerned about being overheard by whatever possible enemy that might be lurking nearby. Force Recon helmets were well enough muffled that any sounds that escaped them were unintelligible up close, and totally inaudible beyond a meter or two. Anyway, communication was via radio burst-transmissions that faded out within two hundred meters—it simply wasn't necessary for him to say anything.

The Marines lay waiting, and watching their surroundings and various detectors for sign of anybody in the vicinity.

After half an hour, Lummus transmitted, "Report."

The four reports came in. Corporal Tony Stein had seen a skinny dog that seemed to be scrounging for something to eat, but none of the Marines had seen, heard, or detected anything human, or even remotely resembling the aliens they'd seen in the images they'd studied on Earth and on the ship. Nobody had seen a body, or anything that looked like part of a body, human or otherwise.

"One and two," Lummus ordered, the command for his Marines to check their first and second objectives. "Record."

"Recording," Sergeant Elbert L. Kinser said as he and and Stein headed for the elevator station's control building.

"Recording." Corporal Anthony P. Damato and Lance Corporal Frank P. Witek headed to the elevator.

After the two teams searched their first objectives, the squad would reassemble and move on.

Lummus remained where he was so he could coordinate the two pairs. One Marine in each pair had a vidcam on his helmet, keyed to his eye movements; the vidcams would record everything the Marine looked at. As a just-in-case, the vidcams had a "deadman switch" arrangement that would automatically transmit their contents to the starship loitering above if the Marine was killed or incapacitated.

The Elevator

Damato and Witek were closer to their objective and reached it first. An executive elevator cab was in its docking cradle. Scorching around the open hatch gave evidence of fighting. The two Marines checked their surroundings and didn't detect anybody nearby except for the other Marines.

"Go," Damato sent. He and Witek went around the cab-dock in opposite directions to meet at its rear. Neither saw or otherwise detected anybody either along the way or once they rejoined. The elevator cab was an oblate spheroid, with three observation ports equally spaced around its circumference, and the airlock in the position of a fourth port.

"Cover." Damato climbed an access ladder to the top of the docking cradle as he gave the order, while Witek remained on the ground watching their surroundings. Another ladder looked to Damato like it went up the elevator's pylon at least as far as the anchoring stays. But he was only going up it far enough to look into the port on that side of the cab.

The cab's interior lights were off, and little ambient light reached inside, so Damato used his infrared scope. All he could make out was the passenger seating and the refreshment console next to the attendant's station, or rather their remains. The interior of the cab was wrecked. He removed his feet from the ladder rung they were on and slid down the ladder the same way he would going from level to level in a starship. That saved his life.

The Control Building

Sergeant Kinser and Corporal Stein reached the control building a minute after Damato and Witek reached the elevator's foot. The building was small. They knew from mission prep that it had two rooms, an administration room and a control room. The former had front and rear entrances, as well as a window on each exterior wall and another into the control room. The latter was windowless, climate controlled, and had no direct access to the outside. The main door, off center on the front wall, was off its hinges, blown into the building. The front window was broken.

"With me," Kinser said. He led Stein in a circuit of the building. They trod on shattered glass going past the administration room; the windows on the side and rear were broken out from the inside. The broken back door was on the ground, also knocked out from the inside. On the way around, Kinser looked in through the windows while Stein checked the area with his eyes, ears, and all of his detectors.

Back at the open entrance, Kinser said, "Inside." The two Marines held their weapons the way a police officer would; finger outside the trigger guard, muzzle pointed up. An infantryman entering a building like this would have his finger on the trigger and the muzzle pointed where his eyes were looking.

The interior of the admin room was a shambles. Everything—desks, chairs, cabinets, office machines—was overturned and broken. Files, hardcopy and crystal both, littered the floor. Using infrared, Kinser and Stein saw stains on the floor, walls, and furniture that experience told them was most likely blood. They saw no bodies or body parts. Looking through the broken door and shattered window to the control room, they could see that the computers and other equipment in it had been smashed.

Kinser and Stein had just turned to enter the control room when they heard the first shot.

Downtown Millerton, Fifteen Kilometers
From the McKinzie Elevator Base

Fourth squad's pod touched down on what looked like a junkyard, but had actually been a parking lot. Corporal James L. Day began recording the instant the Squad Pod dropped its ramp to let the Marines out. PFC Joseph W. Ozbourn began recording as soon as his feet hit the pavement. Land vehicles of all manner were in the lot, every one of them smashed, tumbled, leaning on or piled on others. The Marines headed rapidly for the nearest unblocked exit from the lot to take positions. Day and PFC James D. La Belle went fifty meters left, to the far edge of the parking lot. Lance Corporal William R. Caddy and PFC James D. La Belle headed the other way. They didn't have to go quite as far to reach that end of the lot. Sergeant Grant F. Timmerman remained where they'd exited and watched into the lot.

Fourth squad was on a narrow street, with the lot on one side and the backs of buildings, mostly one story, none more than three, on the other. Doors and windows all along the block had their doors and windows knocked out from the inside. Timmerman was nervous about being so close to so many buildings he and his Marines hadn't cleared, so he only kept his squad in place for ten minutes before calling his men in and leading them into the middle-most building.

The interior was a cavernous space, with only three doorways to smaller rooms; the wall next to two of the rooms was marked with the universal symbols for male and female restrooms, the third with the word "office" next to it. The doors were all broken in. Stains on the floor showed that water had flowed out of the restrooms, though it no longer was. Day and Ozbourn checked inside the rooms while the others covered them. All the fixtures were broken, which explained the water stains on the floor outside them.

A more-than-waist-high counter separated a kitchen area from the larger area; the space had obviously been a restaurant. That was confirmed when the Marines examined the broken chairs and tables—and broken crockery—that littered the floor. The front door and windows had been blown in.

The Marines didn't linger in the restaurant, but began methodically searching the buildings to the right of it. Timmerman always had someone watching the buildings on the other side of the street. Everywhere they went they found destruction; nothing inside the buildings had been left unshattered. There were no bodies or body parts.

They had almost completed a circuit back to their starting point when there was a burst of fire, and La Belle, who was watching the street, pitched to the ground, bleeding profusely.

Jordan, East Shapland

Fifth squad landed a klick away from Jordan, a farming town a thousand kilometers from Millerton and the McKinzie Elevator Base, located on a river of the same name. Like First squad at Millerton, the five Marines dashed away from their pod toward the points of an imaginary star and settled in place to watch and wait. But they didn't spend as much time in observation before moving.

"Up, move out," Staff Sergeant William G. Harrell ordered after twenty minutes in place. He didn't have to tell his Marines what direction they to head in, or in what order to go. Corporal Hershel W. Williams led off, followed by Harrell, Lance Corporal Douglas T. Jacobson, and Sergeant Ross F. Gray. Corporal Anthony Casamento had rear point. Williams and Jacobson recorded. Their first objective was a small cluster of farm buildings about three hundred meters off, on the way to Jordan. They went through a field of chest-high corn. The Marines went at a normal walking pace. They weren't concerned about being seen; they knew how effectively the camouflage pattern on their uniforms tricked the eye, and the rows of corn were far enough apart that they didn't give away their movement by pushing through them.

The first thing the Marines encountered was some kind of native avians that rose complaining to fly away from dead animals they'd been feeding on. The Marines guessed the corpses were dogs, but it was hard to tell; the carcasses had been thoroughly scavenged and the bones scattered.

"Be sharp," Harrell said. He wondered how the crow-like avians had detected him and his men, and knew that their noisy flight would alert anybody in the area to the Marines' presence.

The first of the farm buildings they examined was the barn. It had large double doors. One side of the door was down, the other was hanging on one hinge. Inside, whatever stalls the barn may have held were buried under the debris of what had been the floor of the barn's hay loft. The Marines carefully made their way through the debris, but didn't see anything that looked like human remains, though there were obvious cattle skulls. Elsewhere, a grain silo had been torn open to spill its contents. A shed was broken apart, as were the vehicles it had sheltered before the farm was attacked. The remains of a smaller building and its contents appeared to have been a small smithy.

Harrell saved the farmhouse for last. The porch roof sagged—two of the pillars that held it up had been broken away. The door was blown in, as were the windows on the front of the house. The squad headed for the porch.

The *Monticello* had withdrawn after launching the *Spirits*, and was more than one and a half light minutes from Troy by this time, resulting in a five minute time lag between when Staff Sergeant Lummus at the foot of the McKinzie elevator sent the message that the squads in Millerton were under attack and the message was received by Fifth squad.

"Hold," Harrell ordered when he received the message. The Marines lowered themselves to the ground in a five pointed star, facing outward. "Someone's hitting First squad," Harrell told his men. After a couple of minutes with no further message, and no sign of unwelcome company, he ordered, "Inside, on the double."

The Marines jumped up and dashed into the farmhouse. The interior of the house was as thoroughly trashed as the barn and other out buildings had been. The only differences were that the farmhouse's second floor hadn't been collapsed into the first, and there were no bones. The windows on the side and rear walls were all blown outward, as was the back door.

After a few minutes search, with no additional reports on what was happening elsewhere, Harrell gave the order to resume the movement to Jordan. The Marines kept to the field, walking between the rows of corn, bent low enough that only their heads were above the corn stalks.

Edge of Alberville, Thirty-Five Kilometers West of Millerton

With plenty of space for its relatively small population, the people of Troy revived a lifestyle that began in the middle of the twentieth century, but died out in the first half of the twenty-first: the bedroom community. Alberville had a large enough shopping district to tend to the basic needs of its population of 18,000, and schools from pre-elementary to pre-college for its children. But other than shopkeepers and teachers, people went to Millerton or other locations for work. Commuting was via a network of high speed maglev trains, which people also used to go elsewhere for entertainment, dining, and recreation.

Sixth squad found that the alien invaders had demolished the train system as thoroughly as they had everything else. The guideways were broken and collapsed. The train cars were broken and their parts scattered about. The train station was gutted, and its roof was sagging.

Half an hour after landing, having ascertained that there was nobody nearby, Staff Sergeant William J. Bordelon ordered his squad into Alberville proper. The five Marines spot-checked houses on their way to the shopping district. Everywhere it was the same: front doors and windows had been broken in, those on the sides and rear blown out, the entire contents of the houses reduced to scrap. No sign of a body or body part.

The Marines were confident in the ability of their camouflage to keep them unseen to any observers. Still, they spread out and moved stealthily, flitting from shadow to shadow.

Bordelon called a halt when the squad reached a park that marked the transition from housing to shopping. Again, the Marines examined their surroundings and checked their sensors. Again, they saw and detected nothing.

Until Bordelon gave the order to move out.

"I have movement," Corporal Louis J. Hauge, Jr. suddenly said from the squad's rear point. "Seventy-five, five o'clock."

Bordelon slowly swiveled to his right rear. Seventy-five meters away was a house he recognized as one he'd checked himself.

"They're following us," Bordelon said out loud, while silently cursing himself—how could anybody be coming up from behind? Where did they come from? His motion detector was set to check three-sixty, but it hadn't shown any movement. "Down." He set action to words by lowering himself to the ground. "Show me."

Hauge aimed a pulse of ultraviolet light at the empty window frame where he'd detected movement.

Bordelon looked where Hauge indicated, but the only thing he saw inside the window was the strobing flash of an automatic rifle firing at him. In an instant, he had his handgun drawn and fired at a point behind the muzzle flash. He never knew if he'd hit anything—just as he fired, a burst of automatic fire tore into his right side, shattering his ribs and shredding internal organs.

Less than a minute after Hauge reported motion, all five Marines of Sixth squad were dead.

McKinzie Elevator Base, Millerton

By chance, Staff Sergeant Lummus had been looking in the right direction to see the flash of the weapon that fired at Corporal Damato.

"Sixty-five degrees!" he shouted into his helmet comm. *That shot just missed Damato. How the hell did anybody see him?* he wondered. *I know where he is, and I can hardly see him!*

Damato and Lance Corporal Witek took cover behind the elevator pylon. Sergeant Kinser and Corporal Stein took vantage points inside the control building, Kinser facing the direction the shot had come from, and Stein watching the rear. No more shots came for almost a minute.

Abruptly, shrill shouts rang out from all directions around the elevator. Most of them sounded like they were more than two hundred meters distant.

Well within range of our detectors, Lummus thought. *Why didn't we pick up anything?*

No point in worrying about it, it was time for the squad to get out. Lummus looked to his rear. He was fifty meters from the Squad Pod, but his men were three times as far. If he could make it to the pod, he could pilot it in two short hops to pick them up. If the aliens didn't have something to knock it out before he could get to them. In a few words, he told his Marines what he was going to do. They all said they'd be ready to pile in as soon as he reached them.

"I'll cover you," Kinser said—he had the only rifle in the squad.

Lummus braced himself, then lunged out of his crater like a sprinter leaving the blocks. He heard the loud cracks of Kinser's rifle firing, and the less-loud cracks of the other Marines' handguns. Lummus zigged and zagged to spoil the aim of anyone shooting at him. He was more than halfway to the Squad Pod when he looked beyond it and saw a mass of aliens racing toward him. The speed with which they jinked side to side startled him so badly he stutter-stepped. That was just enough to allow bullets from two directions to hit him. He crashed to the tarmac, dying.

At the rear of the control building, Stein shouted, "I hope he gets here in a hurry!" as he fired his handgun at rushing aliens. "There must be a hundred of them coming at us."

Kinser swore. "He's not coming, they got him." He turned and ran to the back of the building to help Stein try to fight off the aliens. The two fired as fast as they could, but most of their shots missed. The attackers reached the building and dove through the door and windows, dropping their weapons in favor of using their long, vicious claws to rend the Marines.

Damato and Witek fired into the mass of charging aliens from opposite sides of the pylon, but to little effect.

"He better get here soon, or we're screwed," Witek shouted.

"We're screwed." Damato swore softly. He hadn't looked in the direction of the Squad Pod, but he knew that Lummus should have reached it and been on the way by then. But he didn't hear the pod's engine—he knew it wasn't coming.

Downtown Millerton

Corporal Day was the closest to PFC La Belle. He pulled the wounded Marine away from the door where he'd been shot and grimaced at the blood coming from several holes in his shirt. He glanced at La Belle's face; it was pale, and his eyes were rolled up—shock was setting in.

"Stay with me, Jim." Day wrenched La Belle's first aid kit from his belt and reached into it for the self-sealing bandages. He tore La Belle's shirt open and grimaced again when he saw the wounds. Working feverishly, he did his best to cover all of the punctures. Blood welled up around the edges of the bandages. Day guessed at exactly where the holes were, and poked a finger into the bandages in those spots. He got three out of five on the first attempt; the synthetic material of the bandages sank into the wounds and began to do their job, speeding a coagulation agent. By the time Day found the other two holes, blood had stopped welling out and La Belle wasn't breathing.

"I told you to stay with me, man!" Day slapped La Belle.

"Let's go," Sergeant Timmerman snapped, gripping Day's shoulder.

For the first time since he began tending to La Belle, Day was aware of the sound of gunfire from inside the building; the other Marines had been firing at whoever had shot La Belle.

"We're going back to the Squad Pod," Timmerman said.

"Right." Day stood and bent to lift La Belle over his shoulders in a fireman's carry.

"Move it, people!" Timmerman shouted at his squad.

Lance Corporal Caddy and PFC Ozbourn stopped firing out of the windows and followed Day at a sprint to the rear of the building. Timmerman brought up the rear.

Outside, they were almost to the Squad Pod before they ran into trouble. Fire erupted from the building they'd just exited, and the one they'd first entered. The first shots were wild and missed. Day reached the pod and dove in, hauling La Belle as far from the hatch as he could get.

Caddy fell through the hatch, shot in the back of his neck. Day turned back to pull him inside. Then had to reach outside to help Timmerman get Ozbourn, who also was shot, inside. Timmerman suddenly pitched forward with his legs dangling outside the pod. Day dragged him in the rest of the way, then slapped the "close" button to shut the hatch. He crawled over his squad mates to the front of the pod and took the controls.

It was several minutes later, when the Squad Pod was arrowing to orbital altitude to rendezvous with the *Spirit*, before Day was able to turn his attention from piloting the pod to checking the other Marines.

They were all dead.

How did they spot us?

Nearing Jordan, East Shapland

"I have movement, two o'clock, one seventy-five," Corporal Williams said from the point position.

"Hold." Staff Sergeant Harrell's order held his Marines in place, facing outward, weapons drawn. "Moving where?"

There was a pause before Williams answered. "Whoever it is seems to have stopped, my motion detector isn't showing anything now."

"I have movement, nine o'clock, one fifty," Corporal Casamento said a few seconds later. "Approaching at a slow walk."

Harrell thought about it: Someone stationary was 175 meters to the right front, someone else 150 meters away was approaching from the left, through the rows of corn rather than between them. They could be aliens, or they might be survivors. For that matter, they could be farm animals, starving or well on the way to turning feral. He checked his own motion detector to see exactly where the object to the left was. He stood. Using his magnifying face shield, he could make out movement in the tops of the corn in the right direction and distance. A cow? A pig? It wasn't tall enough to show above the stalks. It could be a child.

"Increase interval," he ordered. "We'll take the one coming from the left. Stay alert to everything else. Let me know if you detect anything." He listened for the string of "Aye ayes" that told him his Marines heard and understood. A barely audible rustling told him his men were shifting their positions from ten meters apart to fifteen.

In just under two minutes, the approacher reached them. It passed through the last row of corn three meters from Sergeant Gray. It was bent at the hips, its torso parallel to the ground. It had a short snout that gaped open slightly, showing many dagger-like teeth. Feathery structures protruded from the backs of its arms and legs, ran down its long neck and spine, and formed a jutting tail. It wore leather webbing studded with pouches. It was armed.

Gray and Casamento moved reflexively as soon as they saw it; they dove at the alien to tackle and restrain it. It saw them almost as soon as they saw it, and let out a loud screech as it dropped its weapon and slashed at Gray with talons that hadn't seemed to be on its hands seconds before. Gray screamed in agony, and fell onto his side, clutching the intestines that boiled out of his abdomen.

Before the creature could do anything else, Casamento slammed into it, bearing it to the ground. Lance Corporal Jacobson dashed up and jumped over Gray to get to the alien. He grabbed an arm that was swinging at Casamento, talons extended to rip the Marine's face from his head. The alien was strong, its arm swing sent Jacobson tumbling—but its bones were fragile, and one snapped. It shrieked in pain, and the broken arm flopped.

Harrell dove in. He grabbed the alien's head, twisted it and pulled its neck straight so it couldn't get to Casamento to bite him. Jacobson recovered from his tumble and pinned the alien's thrashing legs. In an instant, he had a tie-down wrapped around the creature's lower legs, preventing it from kicking out. Casamento managed to wrestle both of its arms behind its back and bound its wrists. Then he wrapped another tie-down around its muzzle to keep it from biting.

"The one at two o'clock is running this way," Williams shouted.

"Jacobson, check Gray," Harrell ordered. "Williams, Casamento, get ready." He checked his motion detector, and drew his sidearm, aiming it in the direction his detector showed the rapidly approaching jinking movement.

The second alien burst through the last row of corn and staggered to an abrupt stop, shrieking as it saw the other, bound alien.

And just that fast, the three Marines fired at it.

Two pistol and one rifle bullet struck it. It reared up, stretching its neck high, mouth wide as though to scream. But only a weak *caw* came out. The alien toppled to the ground. Harrell put another bullet in the thing's head.

"I want its weapon and gear," the squad leader said. "Be careful, it might have post mortem spasms." Then to Jacobson: "How's Gray?"

"I think he's dead." Jacobson's voice was thick.

Harrell knelt next to his assistant squad leader. Blood flowed slowly around the loops of intestine that had fallen through the deep gashes in Gray's belly. His eyes were open and glazed. Harrell checked for breathing and a pulse and found neither. He sighed.

"Put bandages on him to seal his gut," he told Jacobson. "Then we gotta get out of here." He looked at the alien that was now bound with more tie-downs, the alien that had killed a friend of his. "Bring the prisoner," he said, gritting his teeth. He didn't say he'd rather kill the monster. But he thought it. He didn't need to say to bring Gray's body; that was automatic.

Aboard the NAUS Monticello, Leaving Troy Space

The Force Recon mission was a disaster. Eight squads, forty highly skilled Marines, had made planetfall. Close to thirty of them had died.

Two squads had been completely wiped out, and their bodies not recovered. Most of the other squads only had one or two survivors; all except one squad that had a survivor had managed to bring back their dead. Only Fifth squad had lost but one Marine. The mission would have been a failure as well as a disaster if Fifth squad hadn't captured one of the aliens.

Who *were* these aliens?

3

The War Room, Supreme Military Headquarters, Bellevue, Sarpy County, Federal Zone, NAU

SECRETARY OF WAR HOBSON'S EYES SWEPT THE ROOM AS HE STRODE IN. EVERY-one he had called for was already gathered around the conference table: Chairman Welborn and Major General de Castro, as well as Army Chief of Staff General John C. Robinson, Chief of Naval Operations Admiral James J. Madison, Commandant of the Marine Corps General Ralph Talbot, Force Recon Commander Colonel Aquilla J. Dyess. Simultaneously least and not nearly least on the military side was Staff Sergeant Harrell, whose squad had captured the alien on Troy.

The civilian contingent was much smaller: Secretary of State Walker sat to Hobson's right. Next to her was Secretary of Extrater-restrial Affairs Orlando E. Caruana. Jacob F. Raub represented both the medical and exobiology communities. Special Assistant to the President Ignatz Gresser rounded out the gathering.

Harrell was the only one who rose to his feet when Hobson entered.

"Seats!" Hobson barked.

Harrell dropped into his chair at the foot of the table and sat at attention, looking nervously down its length at the Secretary of War. He was comfortable enough with the flag officers, but found the high-ranking civilians intimidating.

"Before we begin," Hobson said in a gravelly voice, "I want you all to understand that everything said here is classified Top Secret, and is not to be discussed with anybody not here without specific permission from me or the President. Violation of that will land you in a federal prison so fast your head won't have time to spin. If any of you don't find that acceptable, you can leave now and submit your resignation." He stopped to fix the civilians with a glare. "By authorization of the President, that applies to you as well."

The civilians looked shocked, and Walker opened her mouth to protest.

Ignatz Gresser's adam's apple bobbed as he cleared his throat to interrupt her, and said, "That is what the President said, Mary. He told me himself right before I left the Prairie Palace to come here."

"He can't do that!" Caruana of Extraterrestrial Affairs objected. His normally fair complexion seemed to turn whiter. "That's not—"

"He most certainly can," Hobson cut him off. "He's invoked the Alien Threat clause of the War Powers Act. To refresh your memories in case it's slipped your minds, basically what that means is that Albert Leopold Mills can do just about anything he pleases so long as it has something to do with the alien threat."

"But..." Walker objected weakly, her fingers fluttering at her throat. She shook her head and said more firmly, "I'll take this up with the President when I see him next."

"You do that," Hobson told her. To the group; "Does anybody want to resign?"

They all shook their heads, murmured negatives.

"Good, the President and I would hate to lose any of you." He neither looked nor sounded relieved. "Now to the business of this meeting." He turned to the sole enlisted Marine in the room.

"Staff Sergeant, I've already heard about it from the Commandant and J2, as I imagine everybody else here has. Now I want to hear about it from a man who was there. *What the hell happened on Troy? How did more than two dozen Force Recon Marines get killed on one quick in-and-out mission?*" He didn't sound angry, just baffled.

Harrell cleared his throat, then spoke in a firm voice befitting a Marine non-commissioned officer. "Sir, it was like they were expecting us. They hit us from ambush, except for my squad..."

The basic telling only took a few minutes, then the questions began. Hobson was the first.

"Have you seen the after-action reports from the other squads?"

"Yes, sir. And I've talked to the other survivors."

"All of them?" Robinson asked, incredulously.

"Yes, sir. Every one of them." Harrell repressed a shudder at how few of the Force Marines had survived what should have been a simple in-and-out.

"And you didn't see any people?" Walker wanted to know. "Any of the citizens of Troy?"

"Yes, ma'am. Ah, I mean no, ma'am. We didn't see any people."

"You're absolutely positive that you didn't see any people?"

Harrell looked at her sharply, but his voice was level when he answered. "Ma'am, neither I nor any of the other sur—" He paused to swallow. "Any of the other Marines saw any people." He took a deep breath before continuing. "We didn't see any body parts, either. Although we did find old marks that were probably blood stains." He was gratified to see the Secretary of State flinch—he'd been offended that she'd seemed to doubt his word.

"What about alien corpses?" Welborn asked.

"Sir, the only aliens we saw were alive. Except for the ones we killed," he finished harshly.

"Different topic." Madison's fleshy cheeks and jowls testified to the many years he'd spent skippering a desk. "What did you see of enemy aircraft or space vehicles?"

"Sir, you'd have to ask Commander Schonland about spacecraft. On the ground, we didn't see any aircraft." Harrell saw a question in the eyes of a couple of the civilians, and added, "The captain of the *Monticello*."

"I know who Schonland is," Madison growled.

"I know you do, sir. I wasn't telling you."

A corner of Talbot's mouth twitched, as close as he'd allow himself to a smile at how smoothly the Marine staff sergeant put that overbearing squid in his place. Talbot looked every bit the former recruiting poster Marine he had been.

Madison glared at Harrell, but went stone-faced when his eyes flicked to Talbot and he recognized that he wasn't going to get any satisfaction from the Marines over that enlisted man's impertinence.

Neither Madison's question nor Harrell's answer meant anything at this point; Schonland had already been debriefed by Hobson and the Joint Chiefs. There had been no sign of spacecraft—or atmospheric craft either—in Troy's space. So far as the *Monticello's* sensors could tell, Troy was a dead world, not home to any sentient life, and its space was empty of anything not to be found in any similarly lifeless planetary system.

"Did you see any structures?" Raub, the exobiology representative, asked Harrell. "I mean alien structures, that is."

"No, sir. Only what was left of the human structures built by the colonists. Damage ranged from severe all the way to totally demolished."

"And you're speaking for all the survivors when you say that?"

"Yes, sir. Force Recon Marines take careful note of our surroundings. Nobody saw anything that wasn't obviously human-construction. We have the vids from all eight squads. None of them show anything that could be an alien structure."

"So where did the aliens that attacked you come from?" Raub's Ichabod Crane-like face jutted forward on his thin neck, obviously hoping for something that would give him a clue about the aliens. "Did they have any, what do you call them, dug-in fighting positions?"

"Sir, every alien any of us saw was on his feet and running at us." Harrell shook his head in wonderment. "We have no idea where they came from. None of our detectors picked them up, either, until right before they attacked." He held up his hand. "Excuse me, sir. There were two snipers that fired from inside human buildings. Otherwise, all of them that we saw were in the open."

Raub shook his head, but in disappointment rather than disbelief.

De Castro cleared his throat and asked, "Your squad was the only one that was able to secure any alien artifacts and bring them back?"

"That's right, sir." Harrell took a deep breath to quell the tremble that suddenly threatened to overcome him. "The others had to withdraw under heavy fire." He hung his head for a brief moment, then continued in a strong voice. "The only other Marines who got close enough to an alien to get their weapons or equipment died in hand-to-hand combat."

De Castro nodded in sympathy. "I understand, Sergeant—Staff Sergeant." He corrected himself, remembering that to Marines a "sergeant" had three stripes and no rockers, a sergeant with a rocker under his chevrons was properly addressed as "Staff Sergeant." "You have my most profound sympathy."

"Thank you, sir."

Secretary Hobson looked around the room. "Does anybody else have any questions?"

In murmur or strong voice, they all answered, "No."

"Then you are dismissed, Staff Sergeant."

"Aye-aye, sir." Harrell stood, came to attention, said, "Thank you sirs, ma'am," and marched out of the room.

Hobson looked at Colonel Dyess and nodded—the Force Recon commander wouldn't be needed for the rest of the meeting, either.

Dyess stood. "Thank you, sirs and ma'am." He followed Harrell out.

When the door closed behind the two Marines, Hobson turned to Raub. "What do we know about the aliens, and what were you able to learn from the items that brave Marine brought back?"

Jacob Raub, the NAU's top expert on extraterrestrial lifeforms, made a face. "Not a lot. At least not much of interest to anybody who isn't an exobiologist. The harness is made from leather from an animal that we can't identify, although we're fairly certain it's native to the aliens' homeworld."

"What about the weapons?" Commandant Talbot interrupted.

Leave it to a Marine to want to know about small arms right off, Madison silently groused.

"Ah yes," Raub said with a sigh. "Weapons aren't organic, so they aren't a strong suit of mine." He looked Talbot in the eye, then at Army CoS Robinson. "But the engineering people I gave them to tell me they're not anything like what we have. Their caliber is smaller than 5.56mm and bigger than flechette, partly powered by something resembling a low-power railgun." He shook his head. "Whatever that means."

"Back to the gear," Hobson said. "We can return to the weapons later."

Raub shook his head again. "The harness is stitched together with a vegetable fiber of unknown origin. The same for the pouches attached to it. The vegetable fiber is also presumably from the aliens' homeworld. The stitching is of a type that could have been done in a human factory." He looked at Hobson and shrugged. "Without more artifacts, or knowledge of the place of origin of the harness, there really isn't anything more I can say."

Ignatz Gresser asked, "What can you surmise about the biology of the animal the leather comes from?"

"There I'm on slightly firmer ground." Raub straightened in his chair and leaned his angular body forward. "We were able to secure tissue and fluid samples of the prisoner—non-destructively, let me assure you," he rapidly added when Walker looked like she was about to protest. "We went to lengths to avoid injuring him."

"Are you sure the alien is a 'he'?" Walker asked. "I've seen the pictures. The creature is naked, and it has what looks like a vaginal slit between its legs."

"Yes, ma'am," Raub said, "but body waste comes from that slit, and there is no evident anus. We believe it is more analogous to a cloaca."

Walker nodded. "So the sex organs are interior. Have you seen anything like a penis come out of the cloaca?"

"No we haven't," Raub admitted.

"Then it just as well could be female?"

Raub spread his hands. "It could, yes. But in most life forms that we've encountered, both on Earth and on the explored planets, the males, or male analogs, of most species are the more aggressive, more combative, of their species. Granted, there are a large number of insectoids and piscine species in which the female is the more aggressive, but the larger animals—reptilians, avians, mammalians and their analogs, it's the male that's combative. For all we know, these aliens have more than two sexes or genders. But it's a convenient convention to call the alien a 'he' rather than an 'it'."

Walker turned over a hand, indicating that she was willing to accept Raub's explanation for now.

Raub nodded at the Secretary of State, and continued. "The alien's DNA is, of course, totally different from that of humans. But analysis of the leather of his harness showed that the animal its leather came from is closely related to the alien itself, strongly indicating that it evolved on the same world. The same goes for the threads of the stitching. Naturally, we don't know what the alien eats. However, his amino acids are comprised of the same elements ours are: carbon, hydrogen, oxygen, and nitrogen. Not, of course, in exactly the same ratios. And there are only twenty pairs of chromosomes, instead of the twenty-three that we have. We don't yet know which are the aliens' essential acids, so we don't know what to feed him."

"What *are* you feeding him then?" Caruana asked.

Raub nodded at the question. "We're offering him a variety of foods, both animal and vegetable, cooked and raw. He wouldn't take any at first, but we ate samples to show him that they weren't poison. It's too early in the process to determine which he can hold down, and whether any of them provide him actual nutrition. He seems to prefer semi-cooked meat to other foodstuffs." He looked around, noticing the expression of boredom on the faces of some of the military and non-scientists and decided to wrap up his presentation. "Otherwise, we surmise that he comes from a world with a similar gravity and atmosphere to Earth normal, although his lack of clothing suggests the world might be somewhat warmer, perhaps it orbits closer to its primary." He paused and asked, "Are there any other questions for right now?"

"How has he behaved toward you and your people?" Talbot asked.

"He's been largely threatening, but we have him in a cage and feed him through a one-way drawer so that he can't get to us."

"What about his talons, are they always out?"

Raub shook his head. "Our vid surveillance shows that his talons are folded away when he thinks he's alone, but are extended when he can see one of us."

"Wait a minute," Caruana said. "Where do his talons go when they aren't extended?"

"They fold back along the sides of his fingers."

"That's curious," Caruana murmured. Then louder, "If his talons are folded against his fingers, how manipulative are his fingers? I mean, how could his kind build anything?"

"We believe that when his talons are, ah, retracted you might say, they become flexible. We will have to sedate him and perform a close examination, perhaps even surgery, in order to be certain of that, and to learn the mechanism if they do become flexible."

"When do you think you'll do that?" Robinson asked.

"In the next few days, sir. I can't be more specific. We don't know which sedative will put him under for long enough. Or which might kill him, for that matter."

"The big question I have," Chairman Welborn asked, "is, could this alien, his species, be the ones responsible for the destruction of those seventeen dead civilizations we've discovered?"

Raub hesitated before answering. "Sir, I have no way of knowing. Is it possible? Yes. Is it fact?" He shrugged and spread his hands. "Without considerably more data, I can't say."

"Then it's also possible that they aren't the ones?" Walker asked.

"That's right, ma'am."

"I'd like to get back to the weapons," Talbot said when it seemed neither Walker nor Raub had anything else to say.

"As I said, General, I'm not an engineer or a soldier, I don't really know anything about them."

"I'm aware of that, Mr. Raub. But surely the engineers told you something beyond the caliber and propulsion system?"

"Well..." Raub didn't know what to say.

"Do the engineers think they can replicate the weapons?" the Marine prompted.

"Oh, yes sir! They've already disassembled them and are figuring them out."

Talbot nodded. "Would you be so good as to have them forward their findings to me? And if they do replicate them, I want to see the weapons." He noticed the sour expression on Madison's face and added, without looking directly at the CNO, "We might want to modify our body armor, depending on what the weapons do to our existing armor."

"Certainly, General," Raub said, relieved that he didn't have to say anything more about a topic on which he was as ignorant as he was about the weapons. Yes, let the engineers deal with the Marines.

After that, Hobson looked around. Nobody else seemed to have anything to add, or have an informed question to ask.

"All right, then. The President has already given his go-ahead to launch a military operation to Troy. We don't know a damn thing about what might be waiting for us there. It could be a small force that the recon elements had the bad fortune to chance upon. It could be a major army of occupation. It could be the beginning of a colony." He paused before continuing portentously, "Or we could find a staging operation for the invasion of another human world, even Earth itself." He looked at Welborn. "Prepare a force strong enough to meet any of those contingencies. You are authorized to tell your top staffs as much as they have to know in order to plan the operation—that much and no more, and with the same resignation option and penalty as presented at the beginning of this meeting. If nobody else has anything to add, this meeting is over."

He stood to leave, but paused when Walker asked,

"But where are the *people*, where are their *bodies*?"

"Maybe we'll find out once we get there." Hobson left without another word.

The Joint Chiefs began their planning, but the rest of the military continued in their normal training regimens.

The Central Pacific and Oahu, Hawaii, North American Union.

"ALL RIGHT, PEOPLE, YOU KNOW THE DRILL." STAFF SERGEANT AMBROSIO Guillen shouted loudly enough to be heard over the whine of the landing craft motors and sloshing of water in the welldeck of the Landing Ship Infantry NAUS *Oenida*. "Keep it by squads."

"As if we can do anything else," PFC Harry W. Orndoff grumbled.

Lance Corporal John F. Mackie half turned back and grinned at Orndoff; the junior man was right, the way the Marines of Third platoon were lined up to board the landing skids it was almost impossible for anybody to get separated from his squad.

"Eyes front!" Sergeant James Martin snarled from his position behind his First fire team.

Mackie snapped back to his front, his eyes fixed on the back of his fire team leader's helmet, and continued shuffling forward.

First squad reached its skid and Corporal Harry C. Adriance, the First fire team leader, dropped to his belly to slide in, pushing his rifle ahead of himself. Mackie followed, and found his position to the right of Adriance. Orndoff slid in to Mackie's right, and PFC William Zion to the corporal's left. Martin squeezed in next to Zion. Second and Third fire teams followed under Guillen's watchful eye. The rest of the platoon quickly boarded their skids.

Then all that was left of India Company, 3rd Battalion, 1st Marines to board was the company command group. Minutes later, the *Oenida*'s bow opened like a giant clamshell set on edge, and the skids slid out, into the warm waters of the Central Pacific Ocean, sixty kilometers off the east coast of Oahu. The skids maneuvered to get in line abreast a few hundred meters shoreward of the ship. There they waited, slowly bobbing in the gentle swells, while Kilo, Lima, and Weapons Companies boarded skids and formed waves behind India Company.

On board the *Oenida*, the landing launch officer keyed the final command that transferred control of the landing force to the ground commander, and the four waves of skids, looking like nothing so much as manic, oversized sea turtles, shot toward land at close to 100 KPH. The skids' periscopes, all that showed above the waves, threw up rooster tails of spray. At ten kilometers off shore, the skids cut their speed in half, reducing the height of their rooster tails. At five kilometers, most of the skids dropped their periscopes, making them almost impossible to spot from the beach.

Nearly an hour after starting toward shore, the first wave of skids surged through the surf and up the beach to the edge of the trees of Bellows Field Park, and the Marines jumped up through the suddenly opened tops of the skids and raced into the trees, rifles at the ready.

"Go, go, go!" Guillen and Second Lieutenant Henry A. Commiskey both shouted on the platoon net.

"Move, move, move!" the squad and fire team leaders shouted on the squad nets.

As he ran, Mackie glanced to his right to make sure Orndoff was with him and saw, twenty meters away, the famous trid actor Amos Weaver and the equally famous director Ulysses G. Buzzard. The two were intently talking as they watched the wakes of the oncoming skids as they rose above the surface of the bay. An assistant standing behind Buzzard was taking notes. Beyond them, Mackie saw trid-cam crews setting up their equipment. He curled his lip at the sight, but didn't break pace in his charge across the beach.

Ten meters into the trees, Sergeant Martin called for First squad to hit the deck and take up firing positions. As one, the thirteen Marines thudded to the ground under the weight of their combat loads and put their rifles to their shoulders, looking along the barrels farther into the trees, looking for anything that would indicate an aggressor was there.

"First squad, report!" Martin ordered.

"First fire team, sound off," Adriance snapped.

"Mackie!" Mackie called back.

"Orndoff!"

"Zion!"

"First fire team, all present," Martin reported.

In seconds, all three fire teams of First squad had reported everybody present, and Martin reported to Commiskey. So did second and third squads, along with the gun squad attached to the platoon.

"Third platoon, stand fast and look alert," Commiskey barked.

"What was that back on the beach?" Orndoff asked Mackie as soon as it became evident that they'd be in position for at least a few minutes. "That looked like Amos Weaver."

"Where have you been, Orndoff? That *was* Amos Weaver. And Ulysses G. Buzzard next to him."

"No shit?"

"No shit."

"Wow, I was almost close enough to Amos Weaver to touch him!"

Mackie shook his head. How could Orndoff be so dense he didn't realize Buzzard and Weaver were there setting cam-lines to shoot 2nd Battalion when it made a landing in obsolete armored amphibious vehicles in the wake of 3rd Battalion's landing? How could anybody in the 1st Marines not know they were making an epic trid of one of the major sea battles of the twenty-second century European Union War, and had hired 2nd Battalion as extras? Mackie grimaced; he thought Buzzard should have hired 3rd Battalion instead of 2nd. Hell, everybody in the First Marine Division knew 3rd Battalion was the best in the 1st Marines, probably the best battalion in the entire division. Maybe the best battalion in the entire Marine Corps.

Mackie's reverie was interrupted by Martin's order: "First squad, on your feet. We're going in column. First fire team, Second, and Third. I'm between First and Second. Third, maintain contact with First gun team. Move out."

"Mackie, take point," Adriance ordered. "Me, then Zion. Orndoff, maintain contact with Sergeant Martin. Do you have the route, Mackie?"

Mackie turned on his heads-up-display. A map showing the terrain a kilometer in each direction appeared. Red dots, many of them slowly moving, showed the last known positions of other members of the company. The dot in the middle blinked, indicating his position. A small cluster of purple dots to his right rear had to be Buzzard, Weaver and their aides. A red line showed the route Mackie was to follow in leading the squad. There were none of the blinking yellow lights that would show suspected positions of aggressor forces. Mackie didn't attach any importance to the lack of yellow, he'd been in the Marines long enough to know that the aggressors wouldn't necessarily show up anyway.

"Got it," Mackie reported.

"Go," Adriance told him.

Mackie oriented himself on the HUD map, picked a faintly seen landmark through the trees, turned his HUD off, and stepped out on a meter-wide trail, headed for his aiming point. From here on, Adriance would direct him.

The trees weren't particularly high or very thick, which made for a spotty canopy that allowed plenty of sunlight through for dense undergrowth to sprout. Numerous narrow paths wove through the area. Some were worn by small game and other animals, others by the many civilians who came to Bellows Field Park for recreation—it was common for Marines practicing wet landings to charge up the beach through crowds of startled sunbathers. Because Bellows Field was a state park as well as a military training area, the Marines stayed on paths instead of breaking their way through the brush as they would in other training areas in order to protect the environment.

A hundred meters along, Mackie toggled his helmet net to the fire team circuit. "See anything on your HUD?"

"I'll let you know if anything pops," Adriance answered. "Just keep your eyes peeled."

"Aye aye." Mackie kept swiveling his head side to side, looking into the trees in all directions, the muzzle of his rifle constantly swinging to point where his eyes went. He swallowed. Something wasn't right. He couldn't remember another training exercise where the platoon hadn't made contact within a hundred meters of the waterline.

Then he saw a flash up ahead and froze, with his left hand dropped down and out from his side, palm facing the rear, signaling Adriance to stop.

"What do you have?" Adriance asked.

"I don't know. Movement off the trail about thirty meters ahead." Mackie lowered himself to one knee, looking to where he'd seen the motion, pointing his rifle at it.

In a few seconds, Martin dropped to a knee next to him. "Tell me."

Mackie pointed. "See that double-trunked tree on the left and the mound next to it?"

"'Bout a meter high?" When Mackie nodded, Martin said, "Got it."

"I couldn't see for sure what it was, but something moved there."

"Did you see it?" Martin asked Adriance.

"No. My HUD doesn't show anybody, either."

"You sure you saw somebody, Mackie?"

"I saw *something*. It was too fast, I couldn't tell if it was a person. But it might be."

Martin thought for a moment, looking where Mackie said he saw motion. "All right, Mackie, you saw it, you go. Adriance, send somebody with him."

"Orndoff," Adriance called softly, "you go."

Mackie looked back and signaled Orndoff to join him. "I'm going up the right side of the trail. You go up the left. When I reach that mound, I'm going over it. You hit it from the flank, and be ready to blow away anybody you see who isn't me. Got it?"

"Got it." Orndoff sounded like he had a frog in his throat.

Padding rapidly, Mackie headed for the low mound, keeping his eyes and rifle sweeping over and around its sides. There was no movement and no sound. As soon as he was alongside the mound, he spun to his left and dashed up it, angling his rifle to shoot anybody who might be hiding behind it. There was. Mackie instantly recognized the white band around the Marine's hat and jerked his muzzle up before he shot him in the face.

"Don't shoot!" Mackie shouted at Orndoff.

An enlisted referee was on his knees in front of Mackie. A major with a similar white band on his camouflage cover crouched behind him.

"Damn, but you scared me!" the enlisted referee gasped. Sweat popped out on his face. Mackie knew the Marine had to be scared. Even though the Marines were firing blanks on this exercise, at the range he'd nearly shot the referee, the Marine would have been injured, possibly even blinded.

"How'd you know we were here?" the major asked in a shaky voice.

"I saw movement, sir," Mackie replied.

The major stood up and shook his head. "I was positive we were hidden before you got close enough to see us."

Mackie grinned. "India Three/One, Sir. We're the best." He turned to look at where the rest of the squad was moving up. "Referees, Sergeant Martin."

"Referees, huh?" Martin reached the mound and looked at the major. "Sorry to have disturbed you, sir. Mackie, good job. Continue as you were."

"Aye aye, Sergeant." Mackie returned to the trail to resume his advance.

A couple of minutes later, Lieutenant Commiskey's voice came over the platoon net. "The point just flushed a couple of referees, so you know bad guys have to be close. Everybody, look alert." Primary functions of the "referees" were to determine who were "casualties", which casualties were wounded, which killed, and to free up the "casualties" once it was proper for them to move.

Commiskey was right; less than fifty meters beyond where he'd discovered the referees, Mackie, taking a slow step, felt a tug on his boot. He eased his foot back and looked down, but couldn't see what he'd felt. He took a careful step backward, and lowered himself to examine the path close up.

There! He caught the faint glimmer of a monofilament tripwire about ten centimeters above the ground. He followed it with his eyes in one direction and saw where it was secured to the base of a sapling. In the other it was attached to a flash-bang, a simulated antipersonnel mine. The wire was taut, holding the fuse's striker out.

If the tension on the wire was released by the wire being broken, the striker would slam home, setting off the mine.

"Damn," Adriance murmured just behind Mackie's shoulder.

"Got that right," Mackie murmured back. He carefully examined the area around the flash-bang without touching anything. He was looking for the safety pin; if he could find it he could insert it to prevent the striker from going home when the tripwire broke. He didn't expect to find the pin.

"Pull back," Adriance said, and duck-walked backward himself. Mackie followed.

Sergeant Martin joined them. "Talk to me," he said. Mackie told the squad leader what he'd found. Martin toggled his helmet comm to the platoon's command circuit and reported the finding of the booby trap to Commiskey. He didn't look happy when he'd gotten his instructions.

"Mark the booby trap, then move off the trail to the right and wait for instructions. Second squad's going to the left and Third's in reserve. We're going to sweep the area to the front, looking for an ambush. Do it while I tell the rest of the squad."

"Aye aye." Adriance's expression said he didn't like it either. "You heard the man. Mark that booby trap."

"Right. Mark it with what?"

"Come on, Mackie, you're smart."

"Yeah," Mackie said sourly. "Field expedient. Hold this for me." He extended his rifle for his fire team leader to take. As he returned the few meters to the booby trap, he reached into the first aid kit hanging from his belt and withdrew a field dressing. He stopped far enough away from where he remembered the tripwire was that he wouldn't accidentally hit it, and knelt. While he looked for anchor points that wouldn't interfere with the wire, he opened the field dressing and unwound its straps. He tied the end of one strap to a sapling a few centimeters from the one the tripwire was attached to, then tied the end of the other strap to a similar place near the flash-bang. When the field dressing was in place a few centimeters higher than the wire, he withdrew his bayonet and drew a series of "X"s in the path under the marking, with two arrows pointing at the explosive. Finished, he backed off.

"Here." Adriance handed his rifle to him. "Let's go." Adriance pointed into the brush next to the trail. "You know where it is. Take a position two meters in from it and wait."

"Are you sure?" Mackie asked. "That close to the trail?"

Adriance shrugged. "That's what the man said."

"What about protecting the environment?"

"Just do it, Mackie."

Mackie shook his head. He didn't think two meters from the path was deep enough, and he'd let higher-higher worry about trampling the environment. He went where Adriance sent him and lowered to one knee, pointing his rifle to his front, ready to open fire. Sounds to his right told him that Adriance was positioning the rest of the fire team. More sounds, faintly-heard, were Sergeant Martin positioning the rest of the squad.

Commiskey's voice came over the platoon net. "First and Second squads, move out. Maintain your interval and dress."

The two squads started advancing slowly, the twenty-six Marines walking as quietly as they could through the brush, which wasn't as quiet as any of them wanted. They watched their front for the "enemy," and looked to their sides to check their intervals and dress— made sure they didn't bunch up and that they stayed approximately on line.

PFC Zion, on the fire team's extreme right, eight meters from the path, was the first to spot the ambush. Unfortunately for him, the ambush had heard the squad's approach, and shifted position to face its flank. The detectors on Zion's chest registered the fire aimed at him and his armor froze him in mid-step before he could get off a shot. Off balance, he toppled to the ground.

At the sound of the first shot, Mackie dove for the ground. But before he got there, a flash-bang went off close to his right front. His armor froze and he hit the ground in the attitude he'd been diving; his rifle pushing forward to go into his shoulder, his left arm extending along the rifle's forestock, right arm bending to the side, his legs spreading, his torso curving. He slapped into the ground and the blank-fire-adapter on the muzzle of his rifle skidded into the leaves and dirt in front of him. For an instant, Mackie's toes and the adapter on his rifle held him off the ground, then the weight of his load toppled him onto his right side; momentum carried him over onto his left. After a second, he rocked back to his right side, then left again. It took several rocks before he reached an uncomfortable equilibrium.

Adriance and Orndoff were diving and were hit at the same time as Mackie. They also froze and rocked as Mackie had, until the three of them looked like nothing so much as three upended tortoises.

Before Second squad managed to realign itself and charge across the path into the flank of the ambush, First squad suffered five more simulated casualties. Third squad rushed up from behind and added its fire to the fight.

In the end, none of the bad guys got away, but Third platoon had suffered eight "dead" and seven more "badly wounded," including Commiskey. That left Guillen in command of a platoon of twenty-seven Marines, the strength of two squads plus someone in command. Everyone in First squad was out of action.

The referees Mackie had discovered followed behind Third squad and closely observed the fire fight, noting where all the casualties were. When the shooting was over, the major unfroze them one at a time, noting each casualty's name, and handed the "dead" over to the enlisted referee to escort to the "morgue," where they would remain until the end of this phase of the exercise. Third platoon and the company corpsmen were responsible for moving the "wounded" to the battalion aid station.

A few hours later, phase one of the exercise was finished. All the dead were resurrected, and the seriously wounded were healed. Captain Carl L. Sitter, the India Company commanding officer, assembled his Marines for a debriefing during the hour they had before the next phase of the exercise began. The enlisted Marines gathered in a semi-circle in front of him, the officers and platoon sergeants grouped to his rear.

"Did I tell you to unass your gear?" Sitter snarled. Nearly all of the Marines had removed their packs and load-bearing webbing to ease the strain of carrying the nearly one hundred kilos of weaponry, ammunition, and other items in their basic combat loads. Sitter and the senior Marines behind him were all wearing their packs and gear.

"We didn't do too well out there today," Sitter said after giving his Marines a moment to re-don their gear and start to squirm under his glare. "Things started off well when First platoon found two referees," he looked at Mackie, who looked back without expression, "but went to hell from there. When a company starts off by losing more than a third of a platoon, it doesn't bode well for accomplishing the company's objective.

"And we barely did." Sitter looked slowly over the company again. "As a matter of fact, if we'd been up against a real enemy instead of an aggressor force that was supposed to let us win, I don't think we would have accomplished our mission.

"All right, break into platoons and chow down on field rats. Keep your packs and other gear on, so you don't forget how we screwed up today. Maybe it'll have you doing better on tonight's evolution. And clean your weapons!"

"Hey, what did we do wrong?" PFC Orndoff demanded as First squad settled in the shade of a tree to eat their rations. "The aggressors got us fair and square!"

"Explain it to him, Adriance," Sergeant Martin said.

"You're supposed to be smart, Mackie," Corporal Adriance said. "Tell him what we did wrong."

Lance Corporal Mackie cleared his throat. "We didn't exactly do anything wrong," he said slowly. "It's, well, it's just that we aren't sup-posed to give the bad guys a fair and square chance to do anything to us. We're supposed to kill them before they can do anything."

"See? I said Mackie's supposed to be smart," Adriance said.

"Yeah he is," Martin agreed. "Keep it up, Mackie, and maybe you'll make corporal one of these years."

"Hey, how should we have approached that ambush?" Orndoff demanded.

Martin looked at him, then at the rest of the squad. "I'll bet that right now Lieutenant Commiskey is hearing all about what he should have had the platoon do so that we didn't walk into that ambush. But I didn't say that, and you didn't hear it from anybody. Right?"

Mackie shrugged. "I didn't hear nobody say nothing."

PFC Zion gave his fire team leader a startled look. "What, did somebody say something?"

Orndoff shook his head. "I didn't hear nobody say nothing." He grinned at Adriance, who nodded back.

"Remember that, Marine," Adriance said.

Orndoff grinned, then his expression reverted to confused. "But what *should* we have done?"

Adriance sighed. "Tell him, Mackie. What would you have done?"

Mackie was startled by Adriance again dropping the ball onto him, but recovered quickly. "What I would have done was take us deeper into the trees. That way we would have come in behind the ambush, instead of walking straight into it."

"Oh," Orndoff said, awed.

Every Marine, no matter his rank, or position in a unit, is expected to be able to step into the position of his immediate commander or leader, sometimes even a higher position, and perform well. Unknown to everybody below the platoon command level, one element of the night phase of the training exercise was to test that ability among the junior NCOs and junior enlisted Marines of 3rd Battalion, 1st Marines.

Third platoon was in column in Bellows's Exercise Area Bravo—a less environmentally sensitive area of the park, one that had few civilian visitors—moving toward their objective. The Marines had their night vision screens in place to allow them to see in the dark forest. Occasional flash-bangs went off in seemingly random locations—simulated enemy harassment-and-interdiction artillery fire.

Halfway to the objective, Commiskey called a halt. "Squad leaders up," he ordered on his helmet comm. "Assign your men defensive positions."

While nearly all instructions and data could be conveyed over the net, there was always a chance of enemy intercept. Besides, sometimes a face-to-face meeting was better than remote communications, so nobody thought there was anything unusual about Commiskey calling a squad leaders' meeting. Commiskey led Guillen and platoon right guide Sergeant Richard Bender twenty meters off the path. Sergeant James E. Johnson, the Second squad leader, being closest to the command group, was the first to join Commiskey. Commiskey withdrew a flash-bang from a cargo pocket and tossed it to the side, away from the platoon. It went off before the other squad leaders made it through the trees to join the command group.

"Oh, shit!" Sergeant Martin shouted, hitting the dirt at the flash and the bang. A few meters to his left, Third squad leader Sergeant Frederick W. Mausert also swore and hit the deck. So did the gun squad leader, Sergeant Matej Kocak.

When a few seconds passed without another simulated artillery strike, or any word from the command group, the squad leaders pushed themselves up into crouches and dashed to where they believed the platoon command group was. They found the four Marines gently rocking on their backs in their frozen body armor. Using a few words to coordinate their actions, the two squad leaders checked the downed Marines and their comps.

"Damn, damn, damn," Martin swore under his breath. Then into the platoon net, "Where's comm?"

"I'm here," Corporal John H. Pruitt said as he scrambled to the scene.

"Get me company," Martin told him.

"Right." Pruitt got on the net and contacted Captain Sitter. He gave the handset to Martin.

"Six Actual, this is India-three-one," Martin said in a voice steadier than he felt, "India-three-six, three-five, three-four, and three-two are all down." India-three, Third platoon, three-six, -five, -four, the ancient designations for the platoon commander, platoon sergeant, and right guide. Three-one, -two and -three, the designators for First, Second, and Third squad leaders.

"All seniors in India-three are down except for three-one and three-three, is that right?" Sitter asked.

"And guns. What do you want us to do with the casualties?"

"I've got a GPS lock on your position. I'll forward it to battalion, and they'll pick them up. All right, three-one, you still have an objective to take. You're now acting six. Three-three is now acting five. Assign the senior fire team leader in each squad to acting squad leader. You've got three minutes to reorganize and get moving again. India-six-actual out."

Martin returned the handset to Pruitt and looked at Mausert and Kocak. "It's on us," he said. "I'm acting six, and Fred's five. We've got three minutes to reorganize the platoon and move out."

Mausert shook his head. "I always figured I'd make platoon sergeant some day. But, damn, I expected to have the rank when I did."

"You gonna give your squad to Phillips?" Martin asked.

"Yeah," Mausert answered. "He's got seniority, and he's pretty good."

"Do you have any problem with Glowin taking over second squad?"

Mausert shook his head. "I think he can do it."

"Good. Let's give them the news. I'm giving my squad to Adriance." He turned to Pruitt. "Looks like we've got a new command group. You and me will be between First and Second. Fred," back to Mausert, "you're between Second and Third. No sense in being where one round can get both of us. Matej, keep your guns where they are in the column."

"Sounds good to me," Mausert said. Kocak nodded.

"All right, time's wasting. Let's do it."

"What do you think the lieutenant wanted us for?" Mausert asked.

Martin shook his head. "Maybe we'll find out after this phase. Unless this was a set up."

"Could be," Mausert agreed.

"Let's go."

The four headed back to the rest of the platoon and made the new assignments.

"Mackie," Martin said after making Adriance the acting squad leader, "this makes you acting fire team leader. Put one of your men up front, and move out."

"Aye aye," Mackie replied. He turned to his two men. "Zion, take point. Me, then Orndoff."

"Why me?" Zion objected. "I already got killed once today."

"So did all of us," Mackie snapped. "Move out. I'll guide you."

Zion stepped out, and the rest of Third platoon followed. As soon as the platoon was beyond the place where they'd stopped and lost the command group, an umpire appeared out of the shadows and unlocked the armor of the downed Marines.

"Wait here for battalion," he instructed the four, then resumed trailing Third platoon.

An hour later, not much more than half a kilometer from the position that was the platoon's objective, but still in forest, Sergeant Martin called a halt and reformed the platoon into squad columns twenty-five meters apart, with First squad in the middle, flanked by the other two rifle squads. The gun teams were on the flanks. He went ahead of First squad and called on the net, "Squad leaders up." The three corporals who were acting as squad leaders quickly joined him and Mausert.

"Going for a repeat performance, Sergeant Martin?" Adriance asked with a soft laugh, thinking of what happened when Commiskey called for a squad leaders' meeting.

"Just for that, your ass is mine later," Martin said. After making sure everyone he wanted was present, he said, "Follow me," and stepped out in the direction of the platoon's objective.

A hundred meters farther, the forest petered out into a terrain spottily covered with shrubs about half human-height. In most places, there was sufficient space between bushes for a man to pass without brushing one. Fifty meters beyond where Martin stopped his command group, the ground started slanting upward at a modest angle until it formed a ridge more than three hundred meters distant. The last fifty meters looked to be cleared of shrubs. They could faintly make out bunkers on the military crest of the ridgeline.

"I wanted you to get a good look at what we're facing. Now, most of us have been here before," Martin told the others, "so you'll remember those bushes are thorny. But not all of our Marines have had to make this kind of movement at night. The trick is going to be to use those bushes for concealment as we advance, while not getting hung up in them. The closer we can get to that ridge without being detected, the better our chances of taking the objective. Any suggestions or questions?"

"Stay low, that's all I can think of," Corporal Glowin said. "The trees behind us should hide any silhouettes until we get fairly close."

"Unless they've got good night vision," Adriance added.

"That's why we keep low," Glowin said.

Martin studied the landscape to the front for a few moments, deciding how to proceed. Finally he said, "Go back, get your squads and bring them up. Put your people in columns of fire teams with ten meter intervals. The lead man in each fire team has to find a way between the thorny bushes, so be careful about who you put where. We'll get as close as we can before I give the signal to open up. Depending on how close we are, we'll either advance by fire and maneuver, or we'll get on line and charge. Questions?"

Nobody had any questions.

"So get your squads."

Fifteen minutes later, nine fire teams and the guns were on line parallel to the ridge. Martin gave the signal to move out.

Lance Corporal Mackie looked at his two men and decided he'd take the lead between the bushes.

"Stay low," he said. "Try not to rise up above the tops of the bushes." The same thing Adriance had just told the fire team leaders. "Stay close to me, and go exactly where I go. If you see me flinch, or back up, don't go where I did, because that'll mean I just got stuck by thorns. Got it?"

PFCs Orndoff and Zion said they did.

"Let's go." Mackie crouched, almost doubled over and stepped out. While he looked mostly at the bushes close in front of himself to avoid the thorns, he also looked forward to make sure he had bushes in his line of sight, between himself and the ridgeline. He also checked his HUD to see where the red dots of his fire team were relative to the dots of the others. A few times Sergeant Martin called on the net for most of the platoon to hold in place while someone caught up, or for a fire team to stop because it had gotten too far ahead of the rest.

The weight of his combat load made it difficult to walk bent over below the height of the bushes, and Mackie was feeling the strain in his back after a couple of hundred meters. He knew Orndoff and Zion had to be feeling at least as much back strain, probably more—they hadn't been Marines for as long as he had. He was just grateful that so far nobody in the platoon had gotten hung up on thorns and given them away.

But it couldn't last. Still more than seventy-five meters from the top of the ridge somebody, Mackie couldn't tell who, yelped out loud. The aggressor force on the ridge must have been alert, because the entire line erupted with fire.

"Squads," Martin shouted into the platoon net, "advance by fire and maneuver! Guns, lay down supporting fire!"

Seconds later, randomly spaced flash-bangs started going off on the slope, simulating mortar fire.

"First and Third fire teams, advance twenty meters!" Adriance shouted.

"First fire team, let's go! Spread to my flanks." Mackie lurched ahead, still hunched over. Orndoff and Zion ran to his sides. Zion stumbled into a thorn bush and yelled. Mackie had to dodge a bush himself. "Disconnect and catch up!" About twenty meters ahead of where he'd been when the order to advance came, he hit the dirt and began firing up the slope toward the ridge. But he was shooting blind, he couldn't see anything through the bushes. Over the fire, he heard Adriance order Second fire team to advance. The platoon's fire didn't sound as heavy as it should have, he thought the enemy fire must be effective if that many of the Marines were down, frozen in their armor.

"First fire team, go!" Adriance shouted. "Second and Third, lay down fire!"

Good! Mackie thought. The textbook method of two fire teams advancing while one covered them didn't provide enough covering fire, so Adriance was moving the fire teams up one at a time to provide a heavier base of fire. *Just what I'd do.*

And then he broke out of the bushes onto ground that had been cleared as a killing zone.

"First fire team, down!" Mackie said. He heard Zion drop down on his right and begin firing up slope. He didn't hear Orndoff on his left.

"Orndoff, report!" No answer. Damn! Mackie didn't have time to worry about Orndoff now, he had to place heavy, accurate fire on the positions on the ridge top.

In moments, it sounded like most of Third platoon had reached the cleared area. Even the gun teams had moved up to add their heavier fire. The return fire wasn't as heavy as it had been; the Marines' fire must have had an effect on the aggressor force. But the flash-bangs showing mortar strikes were coming closer.

"Fire and maneuver individually within fire teams, twenty meters!" Martin ordered.

"Fire team leaders, advance your men one at a time!" was the order from the squad leaders.

"Zion, go ten meters," Mackie said. As soon as Zion dropped into a firing position ten meters farther up the slope, Mackie called out, "Orndoff!" but got no reply. He jumped up himself and sprinted a zigzag to drop down a few meters from Zion, and resume firing. "Zion, go ten!" This time, when Zion hit the deck, Mackie didn't call for Orndoff, but jumped up and ran forward. In seconds, everyone in Third platoon who was still combat effective was on line, about thirty meters away from the ridgeline positions.

Martin gave the order. "Third platoon, charge!"

The Marines surged to their feet and sped uphill, firing as they went.

There was a bunker almost directly in front of Mackie. He angled his run to reach the bunker just at the side of its embrasure, firing his automatic rifle at the opening. He reached the bunker, slammed his back against its front next to the embrasure, and jerked a flash-bang simulated grenade from his webbing. He held it for a couple of seconds after pulling its pin, then threw the flash-bang inside as hard as he could. After the simulated grenade went off, Mackie spun around the side of the bunker and jumped into a communications trench behind it. He quickly looked to both sides, but only saw other Marines from Third platoon in it.

He looked at the bunker he'd just passed with surprise—fire was still coming out of its front. He readied another flash-bang grenade and threw it hard into the bunker's entrance.

"With me!" he shouted at Zion, and followed the flash-bang as soon as it went off.

"What the...?" Mackie expected to find bodies, frozen in their body armor. Instead, he found a rifle set on a robotic shooter-mount, still firing downslope. Two other rifles had been knocked off their robots. There were no bodies. He knocked the firing rifle off its mount, and the bunker went quiet. He reported what he'd found to Adriance, who reported to Martin what Mackie had found.

"Third platoon, cease fire!" Martin's voice came over the platoon net. "Cease fire!"

The platoon stopped firing, but most of the defensive positions continued firing downslope.

"Squad leaders, have your fire teams check those bunkers."

In moments, the firing stopped all along the line as the Marines disconnected the weapons inside the bunkers from their robot mounts.

"Does anybody see an aggressor anywhere?" Martin asked. Nobody answered that they did. "Everybody, hold your position. And don't fire unless you actually see somebody. Squad leaders, put your people in defensive positions. And report!"

"First squad, report," Corporal Adriance said.

"First fire team, I'm missing Orndoff."

"Second fire team, all present."

"Third fire team, Kuchneister's down," Corporal Button reported.

"First squad, we have one down and one missing," Adriance reported to Martin.

"Who's missing?" Martin asked after second and third squads gave their reports.

"Orndoff."

"Where's Orndoff? Has anybody seen Orndoff?" Martin asked over the platoon net.

"He's over here," Corporal Thompson of Third squad answered.

"What the hell's he doing with you?" Martin asked, then without waiting for an answer, "Orndoff, get over where you belong!"

"Where's that?" PFC Orndoff asked.

Mackie stood and waved. "Over here, numbnuts."

Martin considered the situation. The platoon had lost four of its top leaders to a simulated artillery strike; he felt they were lucky to have lost only five more in the assault on the ridgeline. "Everybody, maintain your positions and watch outboard—not you, Orndoff," he added when he saw Orndoff drop into the trench, "return to your squad. Everybody, be ready for a counterattack."

"What happened to you?" Adriance demanded when Orndoff rejoined his fire team.

"I got hung up in a thorn bush," Orndoff said defensively. "By the time I got loose, I didn't know where Mackie and Zion were. So I went upslope until I found some Marines."

"Third squad," Mackie said, shaking his head.

Orndoff shrugged. "It was still the platoon."

Adriance shook his head. "Well, you're back. That's better than some." He looked down the slope to where PFC Thompson and four other members of the platoon lay frozen in their armor, awaiting release by the referees.

"Every squad, send a fire team to collect our casualties," Martin said on the platoon net. "This was an automated position. There's gotta be bad guys around here somewhere, so everybody be alert."

It took five minutes to locate all the casualties and lug them, frozen in awkward positions, up to the trench line. During that time, Martin and Mausert discussed what to do next. When everybody was back in position, Martin spoke into the platoon net.

"Listen up! I don't have any instructions on what we're supposed to do after taking this position, but I don't like where we are. The aggressors have to know that we've taken the ridge, and they know how it's laid out. That gives them a hell of an advantage in a counterattack. So we aren't going to be here when they come for us. I'm sending the squad leaders a map, showing where we're going. We move out in four minutes. Bring our casualties. Get ready."

"Fire team leaders up," Adriance ordered. He was studying the new map by the time First squad's three fire team leaders joined him. He projected the map onto their HUDs.

Mackie studied the map while Adriance explained Martin's plan. "We're setting an ambush to hit the counterattack from the flank." A thick clump of trees a hundred meters to the northwest was highlighted, and squad positions were marked in it.

"Unless the aggressors come through the trees behind us," Lance Corporal Mackie murmured.

"We do the best we can with what we've got," Corporal Adriance said. "You got a problem with that?"

"No, Corporal. Just making an observation."

Less than fifteen minutes later, Third platoon was in position in the clump of trees. Adriance had passed on Mackie's concern, and Martin adjusted his plan to have one fire team from each squad positioned to watch the rear approaches to the trees. The platoon sat in ambush for two hours before the call to stand down came from battalion headquarters. A referee came by to unlock the armor of the casualties, and lead the platoon back to India Company's bivouac area.

The exercise wrapped up two days later, and the battalion forced marched along a winding, twenty kilometer route to the Marine base at Kanehoe Bay, where the Marines of Three/One were given temporary billeting.

Marine Corps Base Kaneohe Bay,
Oahu, Hawaii, North American Union.

Early morning

The forced march from Bellows had ended about 0230 hours, and the Marines had immediately set to cleaning their weapons and gear, including the blank fire adapters and hit detectors. After they returned the training gear to the supply sergeants, they showered, shaved, and dressed in clean uniforms for morning formation, after which they were marched to a dining facility for their first hot meal since they left the *Oenida* to make the landing at Bellows.

Back in formation after chowing down, a very welcome liberty call was sounded—most of the Marines in the battalion had never been to Hawaii before, and were looking forward to visiting the beach at Waikiki, and the famed fleshpots of Hotel Street in Honolulu.

"Come on, Mackie, we've got liberty!" Lance Corporal Garcia said. He was dressed in civvies. So was Lance Corporal Cafferata; First squad's three lance corporals usually pulled liberty together. Everybody had brought along a seabag with a dress uniform and civilian clothes. The seabags had been stored in the ship's hold, and brought ashore to the temporary billets during the exercise.

Mackie shook his head. "Nah, I've got a paper due for my Marine Corps Institute course a couple of days after we get back to Pendleton. I should work on it."

"What, more of that Napoleonic Wars crap?" Garcia asked.

"Little tin soldiers all in a row," Cafferata said. "That's all you need to put in a paper about the Napoleonic Wars."

Garcia poked Cafferata's shoulder. "Got that right, Marine! Stand in rows and bang away at each other." He shook his head. "What a damn dumb way to fight a war."

"Come on, man," Mackie protested. "Infantry weapons back then were so inaccurate that you couldn't count on hitting anything at more than fifty meters. Besides, the gunpowder they used kicked out so much smoke that you couldn't see anything after two or three volleys. Standing in rows and banging away was the only way you had a chance of hitting anything."

"Maybe so, but the Royal Marines used rifles," Garcia said. "So did the U.S. Marines. No tin soldiers all in a row for the Marines!"

Mackie looked at Garcia. "Did you ever look at a parade formation? What's that if not little tin soldiers all in a row?"

Cafferata guffawed at that, while Garcia said,

"Point to you."

Cafferata slapped Mackie's shoulder. "Come on, man. Let's go have a few brews, check out some hula hula girls."

Mackie looked at the books he'd packed in his hold-seabag, and the pad he was taking notes on. The paper only had to be a thousand words. He decided that he knew enough about the Napoleonic Wars to knock that out in a couple of hours. He stood.

"Give me a couple minutes to change. I want to try a real Hawaiian mai tai."

Mackie never got the chance to write that paper. And it was a very long time before any of the survivors got to see that Amos Weaver movie.

THE JOINT CHIEFS OF STAFF ASSEMBLED VII CORPS (REINFORCED) FOR THE TROY mission, dubbed Operation Menelaus, and assigned Lieutenant General Joel H. Lyman to command it. The main body of the corps consisted of four Army divisions: combined infantry, armor, artillery, and air. The "reinforced" part was the First Marine Combat Force, which consisted of the First Marine Division, Second Marine Air Wing, and supporting elements. The First MCF's commander was Lieutenant General Harold W. Bauer. The Marines were there to "kick in the door," as such assaults are called, with the Army to follow close behind to do the bulk of whatever fighting there might be. The Navy's transport vessels, designated Amphibious Ready Group 17, were to be escorted by the warships of Task Force 8, under the command of Rear Admiral James Avery. TF8 was built around two carriers, one with four atmospheric combat and support squadrons, and two space fighter squadrons, the other a fast attack carrier with two space fighter squadrons. Ten other warships; two cruisers, five destroyers, and three frigates provided the task force's major firepower.

While the entire force was in space, Rear Admiral Avery was in command. Planetside, Lieutenant General Bauer was in command until VII Corps landed, at which time Lieutenant General Lyman would assume overall ground and air command.

Considering what the *Monticello* had found, or more importantly *not* found, in the vicinity of Troy, and what the Force Recon Marines had encountered planetside, the combined force was considered to be more than sufficient to deal with whatever might be there, the monstrously large ship that carried the original alien invasion force not withstanding. After all, the *Monticello* hadn't seen that ship.

It was possible to covertly assign units to Operation Menelaus, but impossible to assemble and send off that large a force in secret. So as soon as the order to begin assembling the task force elements was issued, President Mills initiated a conference call to his counterparts in the European Union, the South Asian Cooperative, Greater Eurasia, Pacific America, the East Asian Cooperation Sphere, and Man-Home Origin. The first two because, along with the NAU, they were the richest, most powerful supra-nationals; the third because its major component was Russia, a historic trouble-maker that always needed to be appeased; the latter three because they were the locations of three of the four space elevators, all of which would be needed to lift the entire task force into orbit. Simultaneously, the Secretaries of State and War paid personal visits to the capitals of the supra-nationals with the space elevators.

Austro-Pacifica, the Caliphate, and the Junta were considered irrelevant to the current situation, and formal notification of their leadership could wait.

There rose, of course, a furor, with the loudest voices sounding off from Moscow.

Then the dickering started. Pacific America, the East Asian Cooperation Sphere, and Man-Home Origin naturally understood the necessity of the NAU using all of the elevators to put their force in orbit. Just as naturally, they each saw an opportunity to make a massive profit. Accordingly, they almost instantly demanded quadruple their normal fees for use of their elevators. The elevator located on Jarvis Island just below the equator in the mid-Pacific was the only one that didn't require negotiation: the island had been a territory of the old United States of America before the founding of the North American Union, and remained an NAU territory.

It took nearly two weeks of hard negotiating, but everybody eventually settled for double the normal fees. Both the European

Union and the South Asian Cooperative felt it was in their interest to aid the NAU in paying the higher fees. After all, whoever those aliens were, they probably had EU or SAC colonies in their sights—possibly even Earth.

Greater Eurasia broke the news publicly, so President Mills hastily convened a press conference to inform the world at large of what was known about the invasion, and what the NAU was doing about it.

Austro-Pacifica, the Caliphate, and the Junta were considerably put off by not having been notified earlier. But they got over it. Then everybody settled back to watch developments.

Military staffs require constant work. If they aren't planning or running an actual mission, they are making contingency plans. So after standing up the VII Corps (Reinforced), the Joint Chiefs' staff began planning to stand up the Second Army, which would be the largest military force to be assembled under one commander in centuries. Second Army would consist of four Army corps, each with three combined arms divisions. Two Marine Combat Forces were designated to fill out the Second Army. In addition to transport ships, the Navy would provide a battle group with three carriers, each with four atmospheric combat squadrons and two space combat squadrons; a mix of thirty combat ships; cruisers, destroyers, frigates, and—perhaps most important—three dreadnoughts. The Navy didn't have enough transport shipping to carry Second Army with all of its heavy weapons, and other equipment and supplies, so they assumed that they'd have to commandeer a full quarter, perhaps more, of the NAU's civilian space fleets. Not an eventuality anybody looked forward to.

They issued a training order: Stand up the Third Marine Combat Force and XII Corps. After all, there was a possibility, no matter how remote, that the VII Corps (Reinforced) might run into more than it could handle on its own. Together, the Third MCF and XII Corps would form the core of Second Army.

Second-level navy staffers began back channel negotiations with their counterparts in the major supra-nationals that had navies to possibly enlist their aid in transporting a larger force should it prove to be necessary. All hypothetically, of course.

Marine Corps Base Camp Pendleton, California,
North American Union

The Marines of the First Marine Division, the ground combat element of the First Marine Combat Force, were resplendent in their dress blues as they marched, battalion by battalion, onto the parade ground and formed into three infantry regiments, each with three independent battalions; a light armored infantry regiment; an artillery regiment with three medium gun battalions and one heavy; another regiment included three armored amphibious battalions, one armored, one reconnaissance, and the division's headquarters battalion. The division band followed, its drummers beating a tattoo as the regiments and battalions marched in. Twenty-two thousand, five hundred and seventy-five Marines in all. All were armed save the musicians; most with rifles carried at right shoulder arms, the others with sidearms holstered on their belts. As each battalion reached its designated position in the formation, their commanding officers called out, "Order, *arms!*" and as one, the rifles flashed off the Marines' shoulders to be positioned alongside their right trouser seams. Sunlight glinted off the brass of the Marines' buttons and emblems. The splashes of color on the left chest of their stock-collared jackets were the ribbons that told a Marine's history.

Major General Hugh Purvis, the division's commanding general, stepped onto the reviewing stand and stopped front and center to face his Marines. He took a moment to look them over. More than a quarter of them had no decoration on their uniform jackets other than rank insignia and marksmanship badges. Half or more of the Marines had one or more medals; the Good Conduct Medal, perhaps one or two deployment medals, indicating whatever peacekeeping or humanitarian aid deployments they'd been on. Fewer than a quarter of them had the expeditionary or campaign medals that showed they'd gone in harm's way. Not all of those wore the Combat Action Ribbon on their right chests, to demonstrate that they'd come under enemy fire. Fewer than one in ten of the Marines who'd gone in harm's way wore the decorations awarded for heroism in the face of the enemy.

Internally, Purvis sighed. Not one in five of his Marines had looked into the mouth of the cat. He and his officers and senior NCOs had done their best to train the Marines. But had they done enough? Finished scanning his division, Purvis looked directly at the division chief-of-staff, Brigadier General James Dougherty, who stood on the parade ground before the reviewing stand.

Dougherty raised his right hand to the gleaming black bill of his barracks cover. "Sir," his amplified voice boomed out loudly enough to be heard even in the rear ranks of the division, "First Marine Division, all present and accounted for!"

Purvis brought his right hand up sharply in salute, held it for a beat, and cut sharply. Dougherty cut his, then marched to the side of the reviewing stand and mounted it to stand to the left and rear of his commander.

"Marines!" Purvis said, his amplified voice easily reaching everyone in the formation before him. "You have heard on the news, a colony world allied with the North American Union has been attacked." He paused a beat, then continued. "It's true. And it is true that the attackers were an alien sentience—that is, not human. It's also true that it appears that the entire population of Semi-Autonomous World Troy has been killed or taken prisoner. All attempts to contact the authorities, or anybody else, on Troy since the initial alert of an attack have met with failure. We do not know who attacked Troy, or in what force. Nor do we know the strength of any force presently occupying the planet.

"The First Marine Division has been selected to establish a planethead on Troy, to kick in the door to allow the Army to land and retake the planet. We will be supported in this endeavor by the First Combat Support Brigade, and, once we secure space for their operations, the Second Marine Air Wing will fly cover for us.

"We will take this planethead against a foe of unknown strength, with unknown defensive capabilities. We are Marines. We will do it. No enemy has ever successfully withstood us when we attempted to establish a beachhead—or planethead.

"When you return to your barracks, you will be briefed on everything we know about the alien enemy. We are going to respond with full force, and defeat them.

"We begin embarking on Navy shipping in three days.

"We are *Marines!* We always win. Semper Fi!"

As one, the men and women of the First Marine Division roared out, "*Ooh-rah!*"

As the last echoes finished reverberating across the parade ground, he said, "That is all."

Dougherty stepped forward and called out, "Pass in review!"

The division band began playing, its drums, brasses, and skirting bagpipes sounding the chords of *The Marine Corps Hymn*. Battalion by battalion, the 22,575 Marines raised their rifles to right shoulder arms, columned to the right, marched to the end of the parade ground, turned left and left again, to pass before the reviewing stand, their arms and legs flashing metronomically.

Fort Bragg, North Carolina, North American Union

Lieutenant General Joel H. Lyman's chest swelled with pride as he watched the VII Corps assemble. *His* VII Corps! Four divisions strong; the 2nd, the 9th, the 25th, and the 106th. Three of the divisions each had three brigades, the 25th Division had four. Each brigade had one infantry battalion, leg or mounted, one armored battalion, heavy or light, and an artillery battalion. One brigade in each division had a fourth battalion, three of the extra battalions were aviation, the fourth was rocket. And there were the brigades directly under the Corps: engineers, signals, Rangers, military police, and medical. Eighty-five thousand soldiers, his to lead into combat.

Lyman had great confidence in his troops. He knew that he, his generals, their officers and senior noncoms had done an exemplary job of training the soldiers of the VII Corps. He and his corps were ready to take on and defeat anybody who dared oppose them!

He watched his eighty-five thousand soldiers take to the parade ground in their camouflaged war dress. The camouflage pattern was designed to trick the eye into not making out details, or even forms. As he looked out over his corps, except for the faces, he was unable to distinguish individual soldiers; the camouflage pattern blurred them together. Indeed, at the farther edges of the mass formation, the soldiers effectively disappeared from his sight—save for their bare faces.

"Soldiers!" Lyman said in a firm voice, picked up by repeating amplifiers so that every soldier could hear it no matter where in the formation he stood, and never boomed out. "Your time for training is over, now it is time to put your training to work in war. You've heard by now that Troy has been invaded by aliens! We don't know who these aliens are, where they came from, or why they attacked without warning. But that lack of knowledge won't stop us, won't slow us down in our mission to kick them off a human world, and teach them that when they decided to tangle with *homo sapiens*, they bit off more than they can chew!

"You, the officers and men of the VII Corps, are beyond doubt the best led, best trained, most prepared, and best armed military force in history. You are going to perform splendidly, and wipe those aliens off all human worlds!

"When you are dismissed, you will spend the next week learning everything we know about the aliens, what they've done, and how we are going to deal with them when we reach Troy." He paused and, with a chuckle, added, "The Marines are going in first, to be our doormen."

Then more firmly, almost solemnly, "That is all."

Battalion by battalion, regiment by regiment, division by division, with the division and brigade bands playing *When the Caissons Go Rolling Along*, the soldiers of VII Corps passed in review. Lieutenant General Lyman saluted each division's, each regiment's, each independent battalion's colors as it passed in front of the reviewing stand.

"JESUS H...." LANCE CORPORAL MACKIE WHISPERED.

"No screaming shit," Corporal Adriance whispered back.

Master Sergeant Thomas W. Kates from 3rd Battalion's S2 section, intelligence, had just shown them the vids of the attack on Troy, and was now standing next to the projector on the company classroom's small stage, silently looking at the Marines as they digested what they'd just seen. The company's officers and senior NCOs stood stone-faced at the rear of the classroom—they'd already seen the vids and been briefed. Some of the Marines sitting on the benches facing the stage were likewise stone faced—they were mostly squad leaders, although some were fire team leaders, or even junior enlisted. Many, including a couple of the squad leaders, looked appalled, or even frightened. The eyes of a few glowed with the excitement of facing a new and horrible enemy, eager to test themselves.

After a moment Kates spoke calmly. "Nobody knows who they are, where they came from, or why they attacked." That was a statement that had been made many times, at every command level since the word of the attack on Troy was first given by Fleet Admiral Welborn and Commandant Talbot to Lieutenant General Bauer and his top staff. The same statement Jacob Raub had given to the group assembled by Secretary of War Richmond Hobson. The same given by Lieutenant General Lyman to his staff and subordinate commanders. And that statement would be repeated many more times, by officer and enlisted, Marine to Marine, soldier to soldier, sailor to sailor, until nearly all were sick of hearing it.

"All we know for certain," Kates continued, "is they attacked without warning. The defenders of Troy managed to send off these vids and some text messages via hyperspace drone." He paused for a beat before saying, "We haven't heard anything more from them."

A soft buzz broke out as Marines whispered to each other.

"As you were, people!" Kates shouted over the susurration. The Marines quieted and returned their attention to him. "I'm sure most of you are aware of the fact that in human exploration of the galaxy we have discovered evidence of at least seventeen civilizations that have been destroyed by someone, or something. Totally wiped out. And I'm sure you're wondering if the aliens who attacked Troy are the same aliens responsible for those destructions." He took a deep breath before shaking his head. "We don't know. Actually, there's very little we do know that isn't in the vids I just showed you.

"But there is something more." He popped out the crystal that held the vids he'd shown them and inserted another one. "Shortly after the initial data came in from Troy, the Combined Chiefs sent a Force Recon mission to Troy to find out what the situation was. An entire Force Recon Platoon, forty Marines, made planetfall in eight different locations. These are the recordings they returned. Not the entire recordings, mostly just the parts that show the aliens. I've left out the audio on these recordings." He pressed the "play" button and stepped aside so he wouldn't obstruct anybody's view.

The first images that flickered across the screen showed the cityscape of Millerton in the middle- and background, with the idle McKinzie Elevator Base in the foreground.

"Where is everybody?" someone asked, just loudly enough to be heard by most of the Marines in the classroom.

They watched as four Marines in hard-to-focus-on cammies headed for the base of the elevator and the control building. The picture abruptly jumped to show feathery, beaked creatures jinking and jagging toward the cams, firing weapons as they ran. A Marine watching the vid gasped. On the screen, some of the aliens dropped, shot by the Marines recording their charge. Then the aliens were on the Marines, and the vid cut off, to be replaced by the view of a similar attack somewhere else.

By now most of the Marines were shouting, and many were on their feet, leaning forward, hands clenching as though grasping weapons, looking like they were about to charge the aliens. Someone vomited when a cam's pickup was spattered with blood.

"You're cleaning that up, Marine!" First Sergeant Robinson barked. He let everyone react to the vids of the Force Recon Marines losing their fights for a moment or two longer, than ordered, "Seats! And shut up! Pay attention so you can learn what we're going up against."

Less quickly than they had quieted when Kates had ordered them to when they learned that there hadn't been any other reports from the people on Troy, the Marines settled back onto their benches and resumed intently watching the scenes unfolding in front of them.

The intelligence NCO let the vids run their course, from all eight of the squads, ending with the capture of the alien. When Kates resumed his position on the stage and looked at them, he saw something different from what he had before. This time some were angry, others stunned. Then he hit them with what he knew would be a real shocker.

"Eight Force Recon squads landed on Troy. Only one made it offworld with only one dead. Two didn't make it off at all, because all five Marines in each of those squads were killed." That drew gasps; Force Recon hardly ever lost anyone, they were too good at snooping and pooping.

"Now you have a good idea of what we're up against, so I'll give you back to your officers and senior NCOs. Captain Sitter?"

"Thank you, Master Sergeant," the company commander said as he marched to the front of the classroom and mounted the stage.

"Thank *you*, sir," Kates said, and left the classroom. He had to give the same presentation to another company.

"Now you know everything that I know about the aliens." Sitter looked over his company. "Make no mistake, we're likely going to be in the toughest fight any of us has ever seen, maybe the toughest since the world wars of the twentieth century."

Alpha Troop Barracks, 1st of the 7th Mounted Infantry,
Fort Bragg, North Carolina, NAU

Second Lieutenant Theodore W. Greig carefully watched his men from his position at the side of the classroom while they watched the vids of the attack on Troy. He and the other officers of Alpha Troop had already seen them at an officers' call at Tenth Brigade's headquarters. He didn't know whether the troops would also be shown the vids from the Marine Force Recon mission. He hoped that collection of vids wouldn't be shown until the troops were aboard the Navy transports and on their way to Troy. Not that he thought any of the soldiers would desert if they saw those vids, but he thought it was better if they saw them on the way, psych them up for the coming mission when there's no possibility of finding a way to get out of it.

The vids of the attack stopped and Captain Henry C. Meyer, Alpha Troop's commanding officer, took the stage.

"Men," he said, "as you just saw, we are going up against a manic alien enemy. Nobody knows who they are, where they came from, or why they attacked without warning." He didn't know how many times that sentence had been said by officers and noncoms throughout VII Corps, and wouldn't have cared if he did—it bore repetition, and he was certain he'd say it many times more.

"It doesn't matter how manic these aliens are. The Marines are going in first to secure a planethead for us. Let me guarantee you, after those aliens chew up the Marines and spit out their bones, they're going to find out what a *real* fighting force is like. We will make them regret they ever attacked Troy.

There were hoots and catcalls at mention of the Marines. "Hey diddle-diddle, straight up the middle!" one soldier called out. "Show offs!" another shouted. "Marines!" someone cried, and gave a Bronx cheer. "Better them than us," a more thoughtful soldier said quietly.

Captain Meyer let them go for a moment, barely repressing a smile. "All right, all right," he said at last, "quiet down and listen up. Now, all intelligence services, both military and civilian, are working hard and fast to learn everything they can about this enemy. As we learn more, you will be told everything you need to know to help us defeat them. When you are dismissed, you will return to your quarters and prepare to move out. We will be heading into space via the elevators in Kenya."

He looked over his men, seeming to look each of the one hundred and twenty-five of them in the eye, and stepped off the stage.

"Troop, a-ten-*shun!*" troop First Sergeant Powhatan Beaty shouted as Meyer marched out of the classroom, followed by the other officers. When the captain was gone, he said, "Platoon sergeants, when I dismiss you take your men to their quarters and take care of last minute preparations. There will be an inspection in two hours. We will board transportation for the first leg of our trip to Kenya in the morning. Dismissed!"

Barracks, India/3/1, MCB Camp Pendleton, California, NAU

"First squad, on me," Sergeant Martin called when Third platoon reached its squadbay. The Marines who had already entered their rooms came back out to the corridor and gathered with the others in front of their squad leaders. Elsewhere along the corridor, Third platoon's other squad leaders were gathering their men as well.

"Listen up, and listen carefully," Martin said seriously. "You saw the Force Recon vids. An important question that wasn't answered was, how did the aliens spot those Marines? The camouflage of our utilities makes us damn hard to see in the field. You've seen Force Recon in action. Their utes are even harder to spot. Maybe the aliens see in a different part of the spectrum, or maybe they have some other sense that makes them less reliant on their eyes. I hope we find some way of knowing before we make planetfall, because right now we can't rely on our cammies to be invisible to the aliens. Keep that in mind when you're going for cover and concealment—they might still be able to see you.

"Now get into your rooms and finish getting your shit together. I'm going to inspect in half an hour, and I want everything ready to go the minute we get the word to move out. Go."

Back in their room, First squad's First fire team didn't start getting ready for the inspection. Instead, Corporal Adriance and Lance Corporal Mackie dropped into the chairs at their tiny desks and stared wide-eyed at each other. PFCs Orndoff and Zion collapsed on their racks and turned their faces to the wall.

"This is real," Mackie whispered, half to himself.

"No shit, Sherlock," Adriance whispered back. When he noticed that Mackie was trembling, he realized that he was trembling himself, and that the trembling was in danger of overwhelming him. He straightened up and took a deep breath. He looked at his dress blues tunic and saw the Combat Action Ribbon on its right breast, and the two campaign medals and Marine Expeditionary Medal that followed the Good Conduct Medal on the left breast. He didn't have to look at the tunics of his men to know that none of them had the CAR or any campaign medals. He'd been there before, they hadn't. It was up to him to set the example, to keep his men from falling apart before they'd even heard a shot fired in anger.

"Listen up," he snapped. "We're Marines, this is what we signed up for. When you walked into that recruiting office and signed up, you knew that some day you might have to fight a war, might have to kill—or even be wounded or killed yourself.

"Well, we're Marines. We have a long history behind us, Marine ancestors who were always the toughest, most winning warriors of their times. And we're the toughest, most winning warriors of our time. We aren't going out there to get wounded or killed. We're going out there to put a serious hurting on whoever or whatever it was that slaughtered the people on Troy." He carefully didn't mention what happened to the Force Recon Marines.

"We're Marines. We fight. And when we fight, we win. So stop pissing and moaning about what's coming up, and start thinking about how we're going to kick some alien ass!"

"What about what happened to Force Recon?" Zion asked.

"What about it?" Adriance asked back. "Force Recon went in expecting to snoop and poop and gather intelligence. They weren't prepared to fight. We'll go in expecting to kick ass. Now we've got an inspection to prepare for. Get busy!"

Not only did the squad pass Martin's inspection, the whole platoon passed Second Lieutenant Commiskey's inspection which followed minutes later, and Captain Sitter's inspection. Everything they weren't taking, which included their dress blues and most of their personal belongings, went into the company supply room for storage during their absence. Then it was time to fall in behind the barracks and head for the dining facility for evening chow.

The next morning the First Marine Regiment boarded C215 transport aircraft from VMGR 352, Marine Air Group 11, and flew to the space elevator base near Quito, Ecuador, Pacific America.

Transit to Semi-Autonomous World Troy

Even with four elevators operating round the clock, it took time to ferry the twenty-two and a half thousand Marines of the 1st Marine Division the nearly 36,000 kilometers to the geosync station where they boarded Navy shipping. It was a full week before the entire division was boarded and the Amphibious Ready Group in formation to head for the wormhole that would take the Marines to Troy. As soon as the ARG moved off, the 2nd Marine Air Wing, with its aircraft, munitions, fuel supplies, parts, and the rest of its impedimenta began rotating onto the elevators to mate with their waiting flotilla.

From orbit, it took three days at flank speed to reach the wormhole through which they would travel the sixty-two light years to their destination. The sixty-two light years was the quickest part of the journey.

The gator task force was preceded into the wormhole by Task Force 8, built around the carrier NAUS *Rear Admiral Norman Scott*. The five destroyers went in first, followed closely by two cruisers, the battleship that was the flagship, and the fast attack carrier. The TF's three frigates tailgated the *Scott*. Both carriers launched their spacecraft squadrons as soon as they exited the wormhole in Troy's space. The twelve warships *pinged* Troy-space, searching for other spacecraft, but found nothing other than planets, moons, asteroids, and miscellaneous space junk, certainly nothing that remotely re-sembled spacecraft. Rear Admiral Avery ordered a drone dispatched to the ARG, which then flowed through the wormhole.

ARG17, fifteen gator ships—"gator," an archaic term from when humanity was only on one world, and Marines were landed from water seas to land—centered around Landing Platform Shuttle-1 NAUS *Iwo Jima*. LPS-1 was the fifth ship to carry that name. The 1st Marine Reg-iment was embarked on her. Traveling at three-quarter speed, it took five days for the ARG to take station off Troy and prepare to land the landing force. While the gator ships were moving into position, the warships of TF-8 took defensive positions around the planet, covering all approaches, and guarding against ground-based attacks.

Land the Landing Force, Semi-Autonomous World Troy

"ALL RIGHT, MARINES, LINE IT UP!" STAFF SERGEANT GUILLEN ROARED.

"Get out there and get in line!" the squad leaders shouted.

"Move, move, *move!*" the fire team leaders cried.

There was a pounding of boots on the deck and a clatter of loose gear jerking about. Here an "Oof." There a grunt. Elsewhere a curse as the Marines of Third platoon scrambled out of the squad compartments in which they'd billeted for the trip. They scrambled into a double line in the passageway, one line on each side, jostling one another in their haste, and trying not to bump into their squad leaders or the platoon sergeant.

"Squad leaders, report!" Guillen ordered as the thirty-nine Marines settled into position.

"Fire team leaders, report!" the squad leaders echoed.

"First fire team, all present and accounted for!"

"Second fire team, all present and accounted for!"

"Third fire team, all present and accounted for!" came the replies, one of each for each of the three squads.

"First squad, all present and accounted for!" And the same for Second and Third squads.

Guillen clasped his hands behind his back and strode the length of the platoon, looking at each Marine as he passed, his experienced eye looking to make certain every man had everything he needed to carry for the landing. None failed his inspection—all possible failures had already been dealt with by the squad leaders inside the compartments before they fell out.

"You know the drill," Guillen said when he reached the far end of the platoon. "As many times as we've done this, you damn well *better* know it." He looked past the platoon to where Second Lieutenant Commiskey stood just beyond the end of the formation.

"Sir, Third platoon is all present and accounted for, and ready to move out."

"Thank you, Staff Sergeant," the platoon commander replied. "You may take the platoon to its boarding point."

"Aye aye, sir. Third platoon, face aft!"

The Marines pivoted, those on one side of the passageway facing to their right, those on the other to their left.

"Third platoon, route step, march!"

They moved out, not marching in step, turning this way and that as they wended their way through the passageways, up ladders and down, until they linked up with the rest of India Company at a closed hatch outside the hanger deck. Elsewhere on the *Iwo Jima* other platoons and companies were assembling at equally closed hatches leading to the hanger deck until all of 3rd Battalion, 1st Marines was ready. 1st and 2nd Battalions followed in trace.

A clanging from the other side of the hatches announced bosons mates undogging them. In a moment the hatches were flung open, and the Marines surged through, urged on by the "Move move *move!*" of platoon sergeants and squad leaders.

"Follow the yellow lines!" the bosons mates shouted at the Marines racing past them. As if the Marines needed the reminder— they'd rehearsed going through the hanger deck to their assigned shuttles so many times during the past five days they could have found their way in their sleep. Or so many of them claimed. Nonetheless, "Follow the yellow lines!" the bosons mates shouted again and again. They *had* to keep shouting the instruction—sailors think Marines are dumb. Hey, you aren't going to catch squid-boy landing on a hostile planet where he can get his sweet ass shot off. Nossiree!

"Now what do we do?" PFC Zion groused a couple of minutes after Third platoon crammed itself into a shuttle.

"Now we wait for what comes next," Corporal Adriance said.

Lance Corporal Mackie didn't say anything, just squinched his shoulders, trying to make himself as comfortable as he could, jammed shoulder to shoulder against Adriance and Zion, with his pack pressed against his back, the items on his combat-loaded belt poking into his hips and thighs and midriff.

It was long minutes of uncomfortable waiting before they heard faintly through the armor of the shuttle, "Land the landing force!"

Rumbles announced the suctioning of the atmosphere from the hangar deck, followed by the opening of the bay doors. More rumbles and jerks told of tractors moving the shuttles to the launch ramp. With a final shove, the shuttles lost the gravity generated within the starship, and they began drifting away to a distance where it was safe to light their engines. Minutes later, more than fifty shuttles were in formation and began the plunge planetward.

Inside the windowless shuttles the Marines couldn't see the flashes of the barrage the destroyers of TF-8 were laying on the landing zone, nor could they see the atmospheric aircraft off the carrier *Admiral Scott* orbiting to begin their strafing runs when the barrage stopped.

Planetfall, Semi-Autonomous World Troy

The shuttles touched down at hundred and fifty meter intervals five klicks from Millerton. Not all of them touched the ground; some hovered two or three meters above the scrub-covered dirt. The Marines scrambled off, some running straight from the ramps, others having to jump a meter or two from the ramp's lip to the ground. They raced a hundred meters from the shuttles, spreading out and getting on line in squads and platoons and companies. Fifteen seconds after touching down, the shuttles launched, jumping straight up on the downward-facing jets on their undersides. Their combined roars would have burst the eardrums of the Marines, had they not been wearing full-head helmets insulated to block exterior sounds. Still, some noise got through, momentarily deafening the Marines. At five hundred meters altitude the shuttles angled their noses upward and fired their main engines, shooting up into the atmosphere and back to orbit.

By then, more than three thousand Marines were on the ground, in prone shooting positions, scanning the surrounding landscape, ready to repel an assault. In addition to their personal weapons, one fire team leader in each squad used a motion detector, one used an infrared scanner, and the third had a sniffer checking for chemical signs of animal life wafting on the breeze. The Marines watched through the spotty fires set off by the shuttles' jets.

"Ears!" the command came down from Regiment to the battalions when the shuttles' roar was sufficiently muted by distance.

"Ears!" the command went from battalions to companies.

"Ears!" the command went from companies to each Marine on the defensive line.

"Turn on your ears," Sergeant Martin ordered First squad.

"Unplug your ears," Corporal Adriance told his men.

Now they listened, as well as watching with their eyes and their detectors. At first all they heard was the faint crackling of the fires that were quickly dying down, the minor noises made by the Marines to their sides, and the buzzing of flying insectoids. After a few moments, the cries of avians picked up, as did the rustling of small animals skittering through the scrub.

The Marines waited and watched for an hour and then some, while regimental and battalion headquarters launched a dozen and a half Unmanned Aerial Vehicles disguised as local flying animals to circle in ever-widening orbits, seeking enemy positions or movement. Three of the UAVs went directly to Millerton, where two made swooping orbits and the other perched on one of the pylons anchoring the space elevator.

All any of the UAVs saw was a landscape or cityscape devoid of animate life.

1st Marines HQ, Five Klicks West of Millerton

Colonel Justice M. Chambers, the commanding officer of the 1st Marines, listened to the report of Major Reginald R. Myers, the regiment's S2, intelligence officer, regarding the total lack of human or vaguely humanoid forms seen anywhere within a ten kilometer radius of the landing zone. Chambers comm-linked with his battalion commanders.

"1st Battalion, I want you to secure this landing zone until the next wave lands. Once a battalion of the Fifth Marines is here to relieve you, move forward to positions west of Millerton. 2nd Battalion, secure the space elevator to prepare a landing field for the airedales. 3rd Battalion, have two companies sweep through the city to make sure nobody's home, and have one company send platoon-size patrols ten klicks beyond the city. Headquarters Company, move to the elevator and set up in its buildings.

"Questions?"

There were no questions, all the battalion commanders understood the commander's intent. And they all knew that "airedale" was the derogatory term ground-combat Marines used for Marine air units and their personnel.

On the Move, South of Millerton

"Third platoon, saddle up!" Staff Sergeant Guillen shouted. "We're moving out."

"Ah, just when we were getting settled in," Lance Corporal Mackie quipped.

"That's Mother Corps for you, Mackie," Corporal Adriance said. "As soon as you relax, she's got work for you to do." Then to Sergeant Martin, "Where we going, honcho?"

"You know as much as I do," the squad leader replied. "Is everybody up and ready?" He looked along the line of his squad and, by focusing hard, was able to make out that everyone was on his feet. It was a long time since he'd last been discomfited by how hard it was to see Marines in their cammies. He turned to look where he thought the platoon's command group stood and waited for the next order.

"Squads in line," came the order from Second Lieutenant Commiskey. "First squad on the left, Second in the middle, Third on the right. First squad link with Kilo Company on your left, Third squad link Second platoon with on your right. Wait for my signal."

"First fire team, me, Second, Third," Martin gave his squad their marching order. The Marines quickly got in order.

"Orndoff, me, Mackie, Zion," Adriance told his men. "Zion, make sure you don't lose Sergeant Martin."

"As if," PFC Zion snorted. "I don't think it's possible for the honcho to lose touch with the man in front of him even if that man's *trying* to break contact."

"I heard that, Zion," Martin said. "And you better believe it."

A moment later the command to move out came down. 3rd Battalion, which had been on the right side of the regiment's defensive line, hardly had to veer to go past the right side of the area where isolated flames still licked. They skirted the south side of the small city, where the houses and other buildings petered out and gave way to fields and thin woods. India Company, on the left of the battalion formation, filtered through the structures.

On the Southern Outskirts of Millerton

"India Company, check inside the buildings," Lieutenant Colonel Ray Davis, the battalion commander, ordered. "I don't want anybody popping up behind us. Kilo, Lima, slow your pace so India doesn't fall behind."

India Company's First and Second platoons encountered and quickly searched structures before Third platoon finally did.

"First fire team, check it out," Martin ordered as First squad approached a two story, white-painted clapboard house with gabled roof and a porch that wrapped around the near side of the building.

"Aye aye," Adriance answered.

"Orndoff, Zion, look in the windows. Mackie, go around and get ready to go through the front door when I tell you to."

There were two windows on the first floor of the side facing them. They climbed over the porch railing, and the two junior men headed to the windows to cautiously look into them. Mackie went around the corner to the front door, and Adriance took position at the corner where he could cover all three of his men.

"All I see is an empty room," Orndoff said.

"What about furniture?" Martin asked.

"Yeah, it's got furniture. And what looks like an entertainment center. But no people, no animals, no aliens."

"Same thing here," Zion reported. "It's a bedroom. At least, it's got a bed."

"Can either of you see through a door into the rest of the house?"

"The bedroom door's ajar, but I can't really see anything beyond it," Zion said.

"I see a door. It's wide open," Orndoff reported. "Beyond it there's just another room with furniture, and a window on its far side. No curtains or drapes on the window. Not closed curtains, anyway."

"All right, hold your positions, and let me know if anything changes. And keep watch behind yourselves."

"Aye aye," they said.

"Mackie, wait for me, then we go in."

A large hole had been broken out in the lower part of the front door, but the hole's top was too low for a human to duck through without doubling over. The door's bottom scraped along the floor when Mackie, standing to its side, shoved it open. Adriance stood on the doorway's other side. Both Marines had their rifles ready and their helmets' ears turned up. There was no sound from inside the house.

"Go!" Adriance said.

In well practiced movements, Mackie darted through the doorway and to his right, looking everywhere, with his rifle muzzle pointing where he looked. Adriance followed on Mackie's heels and to the left, likewise looking everywhere, muzzle sweeping along with his eyes.

Dust motes dancing in the sunlight streaming through the window on the room's left provided the only movement. There was no sound except for the blood pounding in their ears, and the breath in their helmets.

On the right wall was the open door to the room Orndoff was looking into. Another open door on the left of the back wall led into another room. A stairwell leading up was on the rear wall's right. Another door, ajar, was on the side wall near the stairs.

"Cover me," Adriance said. "I'm going to check that back room."

"Right." Mackie moved to his left front, to where he could see into the back room. It was a large kitchen.

Adriance went behind Mackie to reach the kitchen, staying out of his line of fire, then ducked low to enter the room.

After a moment, he called, "Mackie, get in here."

Mackie didn't run getting into the kitchen—there hadn't been any urgency in Adriance's voice—but still went in quickly. It only took him a second to locate his fire team leader; the camouflage pattern wasn't as effective indoors as out.

"Check it out," Adriance said, pointing at the stove and a table set for six. A pot of something long gone to rot and mold was on the stove. The same was true of three of the six bowls on the table. It was as though the residents had been interrupted halfway through serving dinner, but not so suddenly that whoever was serving didn't have time to put the pot back on the stove.

"Damn," Mackie murmured.

"Cover me," Adriance said, and headed for two doors on the far side of the kitchen. One door was open; it was a slope-ceilinged pantry with a cold-storage unit. Adriance opened the storage unit, flinched away, and slammed it shut again. "It's loaded with organics that've gone bad," he said, and shuddered. There was nothing else in the pantry that could conceal a body, living or dead. He went to the closed door. It opened to a small water closet. Again, no one was in it.

"You know what's weird?" Mackie asked.

"Tell me," Adriance said absently as he headed out of the kitchen and to the stairs leading up.

"There's no blood, no sign of a fight except for the broken front door, and nothing seems out of place."

"You noticed," Adriance said dryly. Let's check out the second deck, and then get out of here." Second deck, not second floor. The Marine Corps was born in Navy ports and on Navy ships, so Marines use many Navy terms.

"Aye aye." Mackie took the lead going to the second floor. Again, he didn't race but still went rapidly, stepping along the side of the stairs so they wouldn't creak. Halfway up the stairs took a turn to the left, over the pantry. At the top, he looked left before turning to the right and stepping out of Adriance's way.

The second floor was smaller than the first, and had three bedrooms. One, larger than the others, had its own bathroom. A second bathroom was between the other two bedrooms, and was obviously shared by their occupants. One bedroom had bunk beds.

"Parents' room, kids' rooms," Adriance said.

"Three kids had to share one bathroom," Mackie said with a shake of his head, relegating the former occupants of the house to the past tense. "I hope they weren't all girls."

Adriance grunted.

They were checking inside the last of the closets when Sergeant Martin's voice came over the comm. "First fire team, get a move on in there, we need to move."

"Just finishing up," Adriance reported back. "We'll be out in a couple of minutes."

That first two story, white-painted clapboard house was typical of what India Company found on the south side of Millerton. No bodies, no sign of struggle, very little out of place, hardly any blood. The southern fringe was like the *Mary Celeste*, a nineteenth century ship found abandoned off Portugal, seaworthy and fully provisioned, with no sign of foul play to explain the disappearance of her crew and passengers.

The heart of the city was very different. It was obvious that a fierce battle had been fought there. Structures were severely damaged, some burned to their foundations. Broken vehicles littered the streets. Unpaved ground was gouged. Blood stains were everywhere.

But there wasn't a single person, human or alien, to be found. Not even a body part. Not even a dog or a cat turned feral.

That feral dog Force Recon saw must have died, Mackie thought.

As ordered, India Company sent out three platoon-size patrols ten klicks east of Millerton. None of them found any sign of human or alien life, or domestic animals gone feral.

A battalion from the Fifth Marines landed in the second wave, escorting Marine Tactical Air Command Squadron 28, and Marine Attack Squadron 214 from Marine Air Group 14; the squadrons took off for the McKenzie Elevator Base as soon as they were off-loaded from the shuttles. The battalion relieved 1st Battalion, 1st Marines and secured the landing zone while the rest of the First Marine Combat Force made planetfall.

Near the McKinzie Elevator Base, Marine Headquarters

LIEUTENANT GENERAL HAROLD W. BAUER, COMMANDER OF THE 1ST MARINE Combat Force, studied his situation board. The 1st Marine Division was all present. Sixteen battalions—infantry, light armor, armor— all ranging out far from Millerton on search-and-destroy missions, seeking the aliens who had invaded the world, and hoping to find survivors. The division's reconnaissance battalion roamed in platoons and squads farther out. The rest of the division was in defensive positions surrounding Millerton and the planethead, formerly called the landing zone, five klicks to the west of Millerton. The 2nd Marine Air Wing was all planetside. Sixteen of the fighter and ground attack squadrons flew cover for the battalions; the other three flew search patterns where the ground forces didn't go. Two of the atmospheric squadrons off the carrier *Rear Admiral Norman Scott* had been deployed planetside and joined the Marine air in searching for humans and aliens in areas not being patrolled by the ground forces. The rest of the MAW's units were assigned to building, securing, and maintaining its base, and maintaining, refueling, and rearming the squadrons' aircraft when they returned from their patrols. The First Marine Logistics Group was busy building Camp Puller, which would be the division's home base on Troy, and in preparing ground for the VII Corps to establish its base when it made planetfall.

The level of the force's activities satisfied Bauer—except for one detail. They had yet to find one bit of activity that they wouldn't find on any habitable world that didn't have human or other sentient occupants. For all he, or anybody else, could tell, Troy was an uninhabited world of ruins, or human structures that would someday decay into ruins.

The report from the Navy in orbit seconded what the Marines on the ground and in the air found: No vessels other than Task Force 8's warships were anywhere in or near Troy's system; Amphibious Ready Group 17 had already returned to Earth to pick up VII Corps. The satellites ringing the planet found nothing but a few gravitational anomalies on the world, not all that unusual for extraterrestrial planets—gravitational anomalies had long been known on Earth and its moon. Troy's two moons had similar gravity irregularities.

The situation was such that Bauer and Rear Admiral James Avery considered sending a message to Earth calling off the deployment of VII Corps. In the end they decided that, in the interest of training for the Army and the ARG, not to send the message.

Wormhole, Troy Space

TF8's two cruisers, the *Coral Sea* and *Ramsey Strait*, two of its destroyers, the *Lance Corporal Keith Lopez* and *Chief Gunners Mate Oscar Schmit, Jr.*, and the fast attack carrier *Rear Admiral Isaac C. Kidd* took up station where the wormhole was about to open. Avery thought, there being no threat in Troy's system, that this was simply a training opportunity for his warships.

An area of empty space, some 400,000 kilometers north of the ecliptic, seemed to somehow shimmer and waver in a manner difficult to see and focus on. Indeed, anyone who stared at it for more than a few seconds was in danger of developing a severe headache. Then, with a *pop* that was somehow felt but not heard, a vacancy that could be called neither black nor a hole in space, abruptly took the place of the shimmering waver and a wormhole opened. A convoy of Navy transports exited single file from the rent in the fabric of space-time; Amphibious Ready Group 17 was returning to Troy space. As the ships exited, they maneuvered into an open formation. The waiting warships took station around the ARG as it formed up. ARG17 now had a quarter more ships than it had before. While there were more than twice as many soldiers in VII Corps as there had been Marines in the initial landing, the Marine aircraft had taken considerable space. That worked out to, man per man, a one-division-one-wing MCF needed nearly as much shipping as a four division Army Corps.

Once the ARG was fully exited and deployed into its new formation, with its five warship escort in place, it began its five-day-long cruise to orbit around Troy where it would land its landing force. When it was three quarters of the way there, a gravitational anomaly on Troy's lesser moon, called "Mini Mouse," which at the time was on the far side of the planet from the warships orbiting in geosync, and out of sight of any Navy assets in the Troy system, gave up its secret.

Sections of the moon's surface rolled aside and missiles shot out. Less than a kilometer above the moon's surface they turned onto a parabolic path on course to intercept the oncoming ARG and its escort.

Combat Action Center, NAUS Durango,
Task Force 8's Flagship, in geosync orbit around Troy

The CAC was quiet and dimly lit, the only light was from the screens of the displays at the various stations in the room, and the dim lights that showed where the hatches were. The compartment felt cavernous, but that was only because the stations were spaced sufficiently far apart that the glow from one screen wouldn't distract the techs at the next. The soft voices of the sailors watching the displays as they occasionally made reports were the only sounds. There weren't even the *pings* that normally would have been heard to indicate radar signals; the *Durango's* radar wasn't on.

"Chief, do we have an exercise going?" Radarman 3 John F. Bickford asked, staring at his display, speaking more loudly than he had when making routine reports.

"Not that anybody told me," Chief Petty Officer James W. Verney answered. He took the two steps from his station to Bickford's and stood over him to look at the display.

After a brief moment Verney called to Lieutenant Thomas J. Hudner, the radar division head, "Mr. Hudner, it looks like we've got possible hostiles heading our way!" His voice cracked. The soft murmurs silenced, and everyone turned to look at Verney.

"Say what?" Hudner asked, startled from his reverie; he'd been thinking of the homecoming he was going to get from his fiancée when this cruise was over. He glanced at the chief to see which display he was looking at, then dialed his screen to show that view seen at his station. It was a second or two before he fully absorbed the sight that met his eyes. Then he got on the comm to the bridge.

"Bridge, CAC."

"CAC, Bridge. What do you have?" came back the bored voice of the watch officer, Lieutenant Commander Allen Buchanan.

"We've got a lot of bogeys approaching from Mini Mouse. They look on course to intercept the ARG."

"What?" Buchanan squawked, his boredom abruptly vanished. He leaned forward and ordered, "Show me." He quickly examined the display from the CAC that popped up on the bridge's main board. "God," he murmured as he slapped the comm button to the captain's quarters.

Captain Harry M. P. Huse awoke instantly and sat up on his bed before hitting the comm button. "Speak," he rumbled.

"Sir, we have bogeys moving at speed from Mini Mouse toward the ARG."

"Sound general quarters and notify Admiral Avery. I'll be with you momentarily." Huse took two minutes to slap water on his face to dredge the sleep from his eyes, and to get dressed.

Bridge, NAUS Durango

"Captain on deck!" Petty Officer 2 Henry Nickerson shouted as the *Durango*'s commanding officer stepped into the bridge.

The bridge wasn't kept dark like the CAC, and routine voices spoke in normal volume. But all went silent when Lieutenant Commander Buchanan reported to Captain Huse, and everybody appeared to be very intent on their duties.

"Carry on," Huse ordered, ignoring the fact that none of the officers or sailors on the bridge had stopped what they were doing following Nickerson's announcement. He strapped himself into his chair, which had just been vacated by Buchanan. As soon as he saw the display showing the bogeys headed toward the ARG, he called to the fast attack carrier *Kidd* and told them, "Bogeys are en route from Mini Mouse to the ARG. Suggest you ready fighters to intercept." He simultaneously transmitted location data on the bogeys and buzzed Admiral Avery.

"Talk to me," the admiral said on his command link with Huse.

"Sir, several dozen, perhaps sixty, bogeys are headed toward the ARG. I have alerted the ARG and the *Kidd*."

There was a pause before Avery said, "I've ordered the *Kidd* to plot intercepts and launch their squadrons. Stand by to protect the Marines on the ground if the enemy launches anything at them. For your information, I have deployed the three remaining destroyers to intercept and destroy the bogeys. That leaves you, *Scott*, and the three frigates to guard the planet. Avery out."

Now all that Huse or anybody else in the *Durango*'s crew could do was wait and watch, ready to move into action the instant they saw any sign of threat to themselves or the Marines planetside.

Fleet CAC, NAUS Durango

"I want to know where they came from," Rear Admiral James Avery snapped, glaring at the display showing the bogeys that were headed for ARG 17 as though his very look could turn them aside, if not actually destroy them.

"Aye aye, sir," Lieutenant Commander R. Z. Johnston replied. "On it."

"Comm," Avery said.

"Sir!" Lieutenant Commander George Davis responded.

"Earth needs to know about this, ASAP. Prepare drones. Launch when ready. Use the wormhole ARG 17 just exited from"

"Prepare drones, aye." Davis began murmuring orders to his section.

Moments later, a barely felt thump signaled the launch of the first drone to Earth. For as long as the wormhole stayed open, more drones followed the first one as the action developed, so that Earth would have the most complete picture of what was happening in Troy space. But Avery knew the picture wouldn't be complete enough, that the wormhole would close long before the action was resolved.

Ready Room, Fast Attack Carrier
NAUS Rear Admiral Isaac C. Kidd

The pilots of VSF 114 "Catfish" squadron were startled by the klaxon that suddenly blared, followed by a voice that commanded,

"Ready squadron, stand by for orders!" The pilots glanced at each other; they all caught that the command was to "stand by for orders," not "stand by for briefing."

Captain John P. Cromwell, the *Kidd's* Commander Air Group, strode into the ready room and stepped onto the small stage at its front. All eyes fixed on him. He looked like he'd just been awoken and couldn't quite believe what he was about to say.

"We don't have time for a proper briefing," Cromwell said as soon as he faced the pilots. "At least sixty bogeys have been detected on an intercept vector from Mini Mouse to the ARG. You are to go out there and keep them from reaching their targets. All available data on the bogeys will be fed into your Meteors' comps by the time you reach them. Lionfish squadron will follow you as soon as they can scramble. This is not a drill. Now get out there and seriously kick some ass!"

"Catfish, let's go!" Lieutenant Adolphus Staton, VSF 114's commander, shouted as he jumped to his feet and raced out of the ready room.

The ready room was adjacent to the launch deck, where thirty-two SF6 Meteor interceptors waited. Sixteen of the Meteors stood with their crew hatches open.

"She's as ready as I can make her, Lieutenant," Chief Petty Officer John W. Finn calmly said as Staton reached his Meteor.

"Is she ready enough that I don't have to run a pre-flight myself?" Staton asked, echoing Finn's calmness.

"If you trust me, she is, sir."

"You don't get to be a chief if you aren't trustworthy," Staton said, climbing into his Meteor.

"I've never lost a pilot yet," Finn told him as he dogged the hatch closed.

"*Yet?*" Staton asked, but the hatch was closed and he hadn't hooked into his comm yet. Well, he *did* trust Finn. He quickly went through his instrument check; everything seemed to be ready and working properly.

"Catfish, are you ready?" Staton said, testing his comm link. "Sound off."

"Catfish Three and Four, ready for launch," came the voice of Lieutenant (jg) Donna A. Gary, the assistant squadron commander.

"Catfish Five and Six, ready," was Lieutenant (jg) William E. Hall.

The rest of VSF 114's two-spacecraft teams reported in as the spacecraft were trundled to the launch tube.

"Victor Sierra Foxtrot One-one-four, ready for launch," Staton reported to launch operations.

"Victor Sierra Foxtrot One-one-four," replied launch officer Lieutenant Commander Alexander G. Lyle, "launch in five, four, three, two, one, go!"

Two by two, flight leader and wingman, the Meteors lunched at ten second intervals. Less than a minute and a half after Staton was slammed back into his seat by the force of launching, VSF 114 was in formation and heading on an intercept vector toward the oncoming bogeys.

VSF 218 "Lionfish" began launching three minutes later.

VSF 114, "Catfish" squadron, off NAUS Kidd,

En Route to Intercept Bogeys

"Talk about your target rich environments!" Ensign Paula Foster shouted.

"Restrain your enthusiasm, Pinball," Lieutenant Adolphus Staton said to his wingman.

"Right, boss. But there's still a lot of them!"

The squadron was closing with the oncoming missiles at more than a thousand klicks per second.

"All Catfish, listen up," Staton said on the squadron's circuit. "We might only get one pass here, and there's many more of them than there are of us. On my mark, give them everything you've got. Remember, every one of them that gets through will kill a bunch of doggies and some of our shipmates. So kill them all!"

Everything you've got was Beanbags and Zappers. "Beanbags" were canisters loaded with sand and fine gravel that would spread out when the canisters burst open, creating a screen that would blast through anything man made in its path. "Zappers" were missiles with proximity fuses; they emitted powerful electromagnetic bursts designed to fry all electronics within a five klick range.

Staton didn't fret over what he knew to be true: that even if the Catfish and the Lionfish killed every one of their targets, at least some enemy missiles would still get through, and there was nothing he could do about it. In a corner of his mind he hoped that the destroyers and cruisers screening the ARG, and the destroyers coming out from the planet, could get everything the Meteors didn't.

Staton checked that his computer had calculated the times of notification so that each of his squadron's spacecraft would fire simultaneously—the squadron was spread wide enough that there would be a time lag before the most distant fighters would get his fire order. Then he paid attention to the rapidly closing distance between his squadron and the oncoming missiles, and noted the vectors each of his pilots would follow after they fired their loads. He was so intent on studying those vectors that he didn't notice that the enemy missiles had launched smaller missiles of their own—aimed at the Meteors of Catfish Squadron—until his ship's warning system set off its proximity alert.

Staton looked at the front display and almost screamed in horror at what his display showed. Each of the sixty oncoming missiles had split into six; instead of nearly four targets per Meteor, there were now more than twenty.

But he was disciplined enough to squeeze his emergency fire lever and send a fire-and-evade message to his pilots. Then he fired off his port and ventral jets to jink up and to the right to get out of the way of the rapidly approaching threat. The sudden change of direction slammed him down to his left; if it wasn't for his harness, it would have smashed his shoulder into the corner of his acceleration couch, dislocating it if not fracturing bones. "Evade," he verbalized to his computer—the closing speed between the oncoming missiles and his Meteor was too fast for merely human reflexes to successfully maneuver out of harm's way. The Meteor's maneuver jets fired: now port, now starboard, now ventral, now dorsal, often in concert or rapid succession. For the next several moments he was flung about inside his crew pod as the Meteor dodged the enemy counter fire, unable to see where his spacecraft's fire went, much less that of his pilots. Or even if his pilots were surviving.

When the jinking finally stopped and he was able to look, he only found five of the other fifteen of his squadron on his first pass. And far more than half of the enemy missiles were still inbound for the ARG.

"Catfish, on me!" he calmly said into the squadron circuit, and aimed his Meteor at the missiles.

"What are we going to do, boss?" asked Lieutenant (jg) John K. Koelsch as he aligned his fighter to Staton's left rear.

"I'll tell you when I figure it out. All Catfish, sound off!" *Who made it through?* he wanted to know. He tried not to think of who was lost.

He got eight replies, better than he had feared although still too few; one was from a Meteor he hadn't seen on his first look, two were from badly damaged fightercraft that could only limp behind. Counting him, only nine of the sixteen fighters of VSF 114 Catfish had survived the initial contact. He hoped that at least some of the other pilots were still alive in the cockpit pods that were designed to keep pilots alive when their spacecraft were killed.

When Staton saw his remaining Meteors were all close enough, he ordered, "Echelon left." The six lined up to his left, angling back from his position. He had no idea what his truncated, nearly out of ammunition squadron could do to stop the enemy missiles.

They weren't closing; the enemy missiles were faster than the Meteors. He gave the order for the Catfish to fire off the rest of their ordnance. Surely the beanbags and zappers were faster than the enemy.

Destroyer Lance Corporal Keith Lopez,
Approaching the Enemy Missiles at Flank Speed

COMMANDER ERNEST E. EVANS, CAPTAIN OF THE LOPEZ, STUDIED HIS SIT-BOARD. It clearly showed three dozen bogeys coming on, with VSF 114 turning to chase them, and VSF 218 closing with the bogeys head on. The range to the bogeys was short enough that the *Lopez* could open fire now and get most of them. But VSF 218 was in the line of fire; no matter how good the firing solution was, some of the 218's spacecraft were sure to get killed by a salvo from the *Lopez*.

"Radar, Captain," Evans said into his comm, "How long before 218 clears our LoF?"

"Captain, Radar," came back Lieutenant (jg) Frederick V. McNair. "At current velocities, 218 will pass through the bogeys and clear our line of fire in twenty-seven seconds."

"Weapons, Captain. Did you copy that?"

"Yes, sir," Lieutenant Guy Wilkinson Castle answered. "Firing solution being calculated. We will be ready to fire the new solution as soon as two-one-eight clears."

As soon as two-one-eight clears wasn't exact; at the distances involved there was relativity to factor in, and VSF 218 was already through the formation of bogeys by the time Radar gave its estimate. What it did was give the fighters a margin of error to clear out of the way of the *Lopez*'s fire.

"Weapons, fire when ready," Evans ordered.

"Fire when ready, aye, sir."

That was before the alien missiles split.

Destroyer Commander Herald F. Stout,
Pursuing the Enemy Missiles at Flank Speed

"They're getting away from us, ma'am," Lieutenant Edouard V.M. Izac said shrilly, shocked at how the enemy weapons had suddenly multiplied.

"I'm well aware of that, Mr. Izac," Lieutenant Commander Jane D. Bulkeley, *Stout's* captain, replied.

The *Stout* was on an intercept vector, but the missiles she was chasing were going faster than she was, and there was no maneuver scheme that would close the distance to optimal range for a firing solution. The enemy missiles would be past wherever the *Stout's* weapons intercepted their paths no matter how the ship maneuvered.

"Weapons," Bulkeley said into the comm, "do you have a solution for hitting those bogeys?"

"Affirmative, skipper," answered Lieutenant Edward H. O'Hare. "It's at extreme range, but I think we can hit a few of them."

"'I think' isn't good enough, Mr. O'Hare. Can we hit them?"

"Ma'am, I'm sure we can hit some of them."

"But not all."

"No, ma'am, I don't think we can hit all."

"Try for all."

"Aye aye, ma'am. I already have the firing solution programmed in."

"Do it."

Seconds later, the *Stout* shuddered as her tubes ejected Beanbags, Zappers, and rockets at the enemy missiles. None of the *Stout's* missiles could accelerate faster than the enemy's, but they could reach a point in space within a fraction of a second of when their targets did. It wasn't likely that the weapons would physically destroy any of the enemy missiles, but the beanbags might damage some of them enough to slow them down, or deflect their courses; the same went for the rockets with proximity or timed fuses. The better chance was that the zappers would fry some of the missiles' electronics, possibly with shock enough to explode their hydrox—or whatever they used for fuel.

Then the tension on the destroyer was palpable as everyone who could see a display watched their ship's weapons heading toward the enemy.

Several hundred kilometers to port, the destroyers *HM3 Edward C. Benfold* and *First Lieutenant George H. Cannon* also loosed their weapons at the enemy missiles.

Destroyer Chief Gunners Mate Oscar Schmit, Jr.,
Approaching Enemy Missiles at Flank Speed

Commander Eugene B. Fluckey, the *Schmit's* captain, gritted his teeth at the view he saw on his situation display. The Meteors of VSF 114 and 218 were doing their best to knock out the oncoming enemy missiles, but already 114 was down to less than half strength, and 218 was being severely punished as well. Fluckey wished he knew the names of the squadrons, so he could pay them proper respect. But he didn't, so their numbers would have to do. It was a pity that there weren't enough of the interceptors to stop the attack on the ARG. Far to the rear of the approaching furball, he saw the missiles fired by the *Stout*, the *Cannon*, and the *Benfold* chasing the attackers. He could tell that many, perhaps most, of the their weapons wouldn't catch up with the enemy.

The defensive weapons being launched by the *Schmit*, and the *Lopez* to starboard and ahead, were taking their toll on the oncoming missiles. But not nearly high enough a price. Many of the missiles speeding toward the two destroyers, he knew, would strike them. Probably enough to kill both warships. Then others would batter the following cruisers, *Coral Sea* and *Ramsey Strait*.

Which would leave the transports of ARG17 defenseless, except for the carrier *Kidd*. And the *Kidd* had virtually no weapons other than her two space squadrons, which were already fighting the enemy.

It didn't matter that the wormhole the ARG had come through had closed; the starships were too far away from where it had been to reach its safety before the attacking missiles arrived even if it had still been open.

NAUS Durango, Flagship Task Force 8, Admiral's Bridge

Admiral Avery helplessly watched the action taking place more than two light minutes distant. At this remove, there was nothing he could do or say to affect the battle. Anything he saw had already happened, any orders he gave to the warships protecting the ARG would arrive more than four minutes after whatever he responded to had happened.

Four minutes in a close-fought space battle might as well be an eternity.

Avery forced his jaw to unclench, his shoulder muscles to unknot. He did it without thought, it was a skill he had developed during the course of nearly four decades of standing watch and commanding ships.

Bright lights that sparked soundlessly in the visual spectrum told of enemy missiles being destroyed by fighter fire. Brighter flashes showed the deaths of interceptors from VSF 114 and VSF 218.

The section of sky short of the approaching convoy suddenly speckled with sparks, the sparks of missiles being killed by fire from the destroyers Avery had sent to aid the defenders of the convoy. But they couldn't kill all of the missiles; there were too many of them.

There weren't enough bright flashes; there were too many of the brighter flashes.

Then came a light that blossomed far larger than any of the missile or fighter deaths he'd already seen—an escort warship exploded, her spine broken by strikes from multiple missiles that had gotten through the screen of defensive fire and interceptors. Then another bright blossom. The *Lopez* and the *Schmit*, the two destroyers in the van of the ARG, were gone.

An even brighter flash heralded the death of one of the cruisers, followed immediately by the brilliant death of the other. Now there was nothing but a few out-classed interceptors left to shield the transports of Amphibious Ready Group 17—and they were chasing the missiles.

Avery didn't allow himself to hang his head; he continued to watch the displays. In another place and time, a fleet commander in his situation would retire to his cabin and commit ritual suicide. But in the here and now, he remained alive and in command, doing whatever he could to salvage the situation, until another admiral arrived from Earth to relieve him.

"Fleet CAC," he demanded into his comm, "have you found where they come from yet?"

"Sir, we know they came from behind Mini Mouse. We're analyzing their trajectory to determine exactly where. We should have the location shortly."

"Keep me informed."

"Aye aye, sir."

NAUS Durango, Fleet Combat Action Center

Lieutenant Commander R. Z. Johnston scowled, visibly upset that the enemy had sneaked an attack past him. He already had his people back-tracking the trajectory of the missiles to determine exactly where they originated. They came from the far side of Mini Mouse, that much was obvious. The small moon wasn't tidally locked to Troy, so the launch site had moved since the missiles went up. That meant the launch site—sites?—had moved, relative to where the moon's "far side" was now. Elementary to calculate. And they had a complete map of the surface of the small moon. Two analysts were examining the maps, and one of them was plotting the possible site/sites against known gravitational anomalies.

Johnston suspected the launch site was on or just below, the surface put in place after the initial attack. He didn't see any way they could have brought in the heavy equipment they'd need to dig in deeply without being noticed from the planet's surface—or the digging operations noticed by approaching starships even if they were able to shield the operation from surface-based observers on Troy—before the original attack. *Ergo*, Johnston concluded, *the site must be on or near the surface, and camouflaged.*

It was just too bad Mini Mouse hadn't been thoroughly mapped earlier. Then it would have been an easy job to compare that against the navy's maps that showed what was there now.

"Sir," Senior Chief John C. McCloy interrupted Johnston's thoughts, "I think we've hit paydirt."

"Show me."

McCloy toggled one of the analyst's displays to the CAC head's display. It showed four surface soft spots with something with variable density immediately below.

"Bingo," Johnston murmured. "Admiral's bridge, CAC."

Avery was waiting for the call. "Speak to me."

"Sir, we've got four probable targets. Each shows distinct features of camouflaged artillery positions."

"Can their locations be hit by the *Scott* or the *Durango*?"

"Negative, sir." He looked at McCloy.

"Working on it," McCloy said softly, and turned to the analysts to get them to work on initial plots to move the two warships into position to strike the enemy sites.

"Sir, we are working on vectors for *Scott* and *Durango* to take to be able to strike at the Mini Mouse sites."

"Keep doing it. Let me know when you have the vectors. I'll order them to follow them, and have their CACs coordinate with you. Avery out."

NAUS *Peleliu*, Flagship of Amphibious Ready Group 17, Commodore's Bridge

Rear Admiral Daniel J. Callaghan, commanding ARG 17, and Lieutenant General Joel H. Lyman, commanding VII Corps, stood at the control bar separating the commodore's station from the officers overseeing the fleet's operations. The main display that hovered before them showed a ninety-light-second-diameter, three dimensional sphere to their front. Callaghan was in his crisp khaki duty uniform. Lyman, who a short time earlier had expected to be making planetfall in his corps' second wave, was in his eye-fooling camouflage field uniform. Where their arms almost touched, Lyman's nearly blended visually into Callaghan's.

Callaghan's mouth was dry. It didn't take any understanding of orbital mechanics to see that Catfish and Lionfish squadrons— what was left of them—had virtually no chance of destroying any of the fifty-eight missiles still homing in on the nineteen transports and supply ships of ARG17, and that most if not all of the starships of ARG17 were going to be hit, possibly—probably—killed. Even a six-year-old playing "Deep Space Fleet" on a child-size HUD could see that.

His only consolation was that he probably wouldn't survive to face a board of inquiry.

He'd long since given the order for his starships to take evasive action, maneuvering in patterns of random movement; he knew it was a feeble attempt to trick the oncoming missiles into missing them, but it was better than nothing. Starships, particularly the transports and support vessels of a gator navy, don't maneuver very nimbly. Feeble or not, the maneuvering might save some of his ships—and the troops they carried.

His mouth was dry, but he stood erect, hands clasped in the small of his back, head held high, expression neutral. He didn't look like a man facing imminent death. Next to him, he barely heard General Lyman murmuring; likely prayers to whatever god he might believe in.

On the main display two icons, representing Landing Platform, Shuttle, LPS8 *Phillips Head* and the logistics support ship *Richmond* merged, then shattered into pieces scattering away.

There goes several hundred sailors and an army brigade, Callaghan thought grimly.

The *Phillips Head* and the *Richmond* hadn't been hit by enemy fire; they'd collided with each other.

Lyman emitted a groan and squeezed his eyes shut.

Seconds later, the oncoming enemy weapons began impacting the starships of his flotilla. Callaghan didn't look away from the main display; he owed the officers and men of ARG17 and VII Corps that much respect. He saw four missiles strike the amphibious landing ferry *Yorktown*, breaking her in two. He watched two missiles hit the amphibious landing dock *Saratoga,* not death-dealing hits, but certainly crippling. The *Grandar Bay* was staggered by one hit. The escort carrier *Kidd* was pummeled by three missiles; Callaghan wondered if she would be able to retrieve her Meteor pilots—if any of them had survived. He only saw one missile strike the *Kandahar*, but she exploded—the missile must have found its way to the power plant.

There were hits on more of the starships of ARG 17, but Callaghan didn't see them. He spent his last seconds standing at attention as he watched five missiles close on the *Peleliu*.

Rear Admiral Callaghan died with his eyes open. Lieutenant General Lyman opened his eyes in time to die the same way.

Before the now-hear-this message even finished its first go-through, Second Lieutenant Theodore W. Greig bolted from the officers mess and raced, twisting side to side to avoid collisions with sailors and soldiers going in the opposite direction in the narrow passageways, to the compartment where his platoon was quartered on the amphibious assault ship.

"Sergeant Quinn," he huffed into his comm unit, "where are you? I'm heading for the platoon."

"I'm almost there, LT. I already put out a call for everyone to report in."

"Thanks, Sergeant."

"Hey, it's what a platoon sergeant does."

"The good ones, anyway." Greig snapped his comm off and twisted past a last few sailors before he reached the door to his platoon's compartment and headed in. A glance showed him that Quinn had just arrived, and only two or three of his soldiers weren't present.

"'Toon, a-ten-*hut!*" Quinn bellowed when the officer entered.

Greig gave his men a few seconds to come to their feet and begin moving into the posture of attention before shouting, "At ease!" He turned and stepped aside at the sound of thudding footsteps in the passageway behind himself, just in time to dodge two soldiers who grabbed the doorway combing and spun into the compartment.

"Is that everybody?" he asked.

Quinn had already called for a squad leaders' report. In seconds, he had it. "Second platoon, all present and accounted for," he barked.

Greig nodded. "Good," he said, then took a couple of seconds to organize his thoughts. "As you just heard on the *Juno Beach's* PA system, the fleet is under attack. That's *this* fleet, including the ship we're on. There are two fleets, the troop transfer fleet we're in, and a warship fleet. The warships are fighting off the attackers. But, if history's any indication, some of the attackers are going to be successful." He paused to let that sink in. "What this means in practical terms, is the *Juno Beach* might get hit, maybe even destroyed." He had to raise his hands and voice to quell the tumult that rose.

Quinn's roars of "Knock it off and listen up!" probably had more to do with the sudden silence than the lieutenant's shout.

"Yes," Greig snapped. "That means we could all get killed before we even make planetfall. But—" He again had to call for quiet. "But it doesn't mean that we *will* get killed. First, because the enemy might not hit this ship. Second, because there are stasis stations available. We are going to one. All of Second platoon. If the *Juno Beach* gets hit, even destroyed, we'll be safe until we get rescued and brought out of stasis. If we don't get hit at all, we're still safe and alive until someone releases us from stasis.

Sergeant Quinn and I know where the nearest stasis station is. We are going to take you there now and we are all going into stasis. We'll be out of the way of the ship's crew, and we'll be safe in case the *Juno Beach* gets hit. You've all been through a stasis drill, so you know how it's done. Squad leaders, get your troops together, and follow Sergeant Quinn." He nodded at his platoon sergeant. "Lead the way."

Second platoon of Alpha Troop, First of the Seventh Mounted Infantry, 10th Brigade, headed to the nearest stasis station, which was close enough that the lead soldier entered it before the last soldier left the platoon's compartment.

It took less than fifteen minutes for the twenty-four troops of the platoon to get into the individual units, hooked up, and checked by their squad leaders. Greig and Quinn checked the squad leaders.

Before they got into their units, Quinn asked, "LT., did the captain tell all the platoon commanders to head for stasis?"

Greig looked his platoon sergeant in the eye and said quietly, "You can't get in trouble for what you don't know. Remember that, just in case I'm wrong."

NAUS Durango, Admiral's Bridge

"If it pleases Captain Huse, I would like to speak with him," Rear Admiral James Avery said into his comm. Task Force 8 belonged to Avery, but the *Durango* belonged to Huse, and his position must be acknowledged.

"Huse here, Admiral," the captain's voice came back seconds later.

"Captain," Avery said, calling him by his rank rather than his given name as he normally would to make totally clear that he was giving orders, "thanks for getting back to me so quickly." As if there was any doubt that a captain wouldn't answer an admiral's call as fast as possible. "Those bogeys attacking the ARG came from Mini Mouse. Fleet CAC has identified their points of origin. I want you to maneuver into a position where you can continue giving cover to the planetside Marines, and simultaneously fire on the moon. Have your CAC coordinate with mine." The *Durango's* Combat Action Center directed the ship's fight; the Fleet CAC coordinated the fight of two or more of the fleet's ships. "I'm sending the *Scott* to attack the identified locations from where the enemy launched its missiles. When you are in position, I will send further orders to *Durango* and *Scott* to coordinate your attacks.

"Questions?"

"Negative, sir. I will inform the admiral the instant I am in position."

"Thank you, Captain." Avery broke the connection, and settled back to watch developments.

NAUS Durango, Bridge

"Comm," Huse said to Lieutenant Commander George F. Davis, his communications officer, "get me CAC."

"CAC, aye, sir," Davis answered.

Seconds later; "CAC, Lieutenant Hudner, sir."

"Mr. Hudner, has Fleet CAC given you the locations on Mini Mouse the enemy fired from?"

"Yes, sir. They are coming in now."

"Good man. The admiral is about to order a counterattack. Make a priority list with coordinates for bombardment, and send it to me instantly. Remember, we have to maintain cover for the Marines planetside."

"Aye aye. sir, you will have it immediately."

NAUS Durango, Admiral's Bridge

While Huse was giving orders to his CAC, Avery was in communication with Captain William R. Rush, skipper of the *Scott*. The *Scott* and the *Durango* were two of the most powerful warships in the NAU Navy, and the most powerful in TF8.

It took several seconds longer for Rush to answer Avery's call than it had Huse, during which time the plot arrived from the CAC. But Huse was on the same starship as Avery, while Rush on the *Scott* was more than 100,000 kilometers distant; in space, distance equals time.

"*Scott* Actual here, Sir." Rush's voice when it came was clear and crisp. Identifying himself by position rather than name indicated that he anticipated that he was about to receive action orders.

"*Scott* Actual, I believe that you are in a position from which you can launch Kestrel strikes on Mini Mouse."

Seconds later Rush replied, "That's affirmative, sir."

"Be advised, the *Durango* is maneuvering into position to strike targets on Mini Mouse. When she is in position, I will give orders to the two of you to coordinate your attacks. In the meantime, launch your squadrons and have them take up parking orbits on the limb of Mini Mouse, where they will wait for orders to strike at these targets which have been identified by Fleet CAC." He pressed a "transmit" button to send the plot to the *Scott*.

"Sir, *Scott* maneuvering to launch Kestrels.

"Launch as soon as you are ready, *Scott*."

MINI MOUSE'S ROTATION HAD MOVED THE LIKELY LAUNCH SITES IDENTIFIED BY fleet CAC from opposite Troy to halfway to its limb. Troy had likewise rotated but, with a longer rotation period, not as far around its axis. The *Durango* moved far enough to fire on the moon that was still out of sight beyond the edge of Troy, while staying where she could give the Marines on the ground fire support should they need it.

Lieutenant Thomas Hudner and his crew in the *Durango*'s CAC watched over their computers while they calculated firing solutions for the ship's weapons to hit the probable locations of the alien launch sites. It would be nearly impossible for ballistic weapons to make the strikes, but simple for the *Durango*'s—once it was in position. Right now, it was covering the Marines planetside.

"Got it!" Senior Chief Petty Officer Francis Edward Ormsbee exclaimed.

"Show me, Francis Edward," Hudner said, stepping to the man everybody from petty officer first class on up called "Francis Edward."

"Ya see, Mr. T—" Ormsbee called everybody except Captain Huse and the admiral whatever he wanted to. "—we got the jarheads covered right there," he pointed at a group of lines on the schematic he'd just put together, "an' the mizzuls came from there. We can hit 'em from where we are." He looked at his division commander. "Don'cha think ya oughtta tell the skipper?"

"Well now, Francis Edward, I think that might be a good idea. A very good idea indeed."

Hudner notified Captain Huse, who in turn informed Admiral Avery, and two minutes later, the *Durango* fired a barrage of missiles programmed to loop around the side of the side of the planet and then swing past the limb of Mini Mouse, to impact at four locations on the moon's far side.

Four AV16(E) Kestrels followed behind to get visual confirmation of the strikes.

VSFA 132, "Piranha" squadron off NAUS Scott,
En Route from Parking Orbit to Target

"Nibblers, Nibblers, all Nibblers, this is Big Teeth. Answer up," Lieutenant Commander Georgia Street said into her squadron circuit. "Verify that you have your strike coordinates and path programmed into your comps."

She watched as her board lit up with replies. All four of the squadron's four fighter-attack craft divisions were properly aligned to bombard their assigned targets, each division coming in from a different direction. Scatter-Blast cluster bombs fired by sixteen craft from two thousand meters altitude. The divisions would loose their loads at ten-second intervals. The Blasters were set to go off one hundred meters above the surface, scattering their munitions over a ten-by-ten-kilometer area, shredding the camouflage coverings to confetti, churning the regolith all the way to the bedrock like a brutally plowed field. If anything was still under the camouflage, it would be obliterated. As soon as their bombs dropped, the AV16C Kestrels' flight paths called for them to shoot into a vertical arabesques, designed to allow them to avoid both each other and the debris blasting up from the surface with margins of safety.

"We aren't going to have much time on our approach," Street continued in a pep-talk tone, "but Piranha squadron is the best in the Navy, and that means nobody can do this job better. So let's get this thing done!"

Not much time indeed. They were speeding around Mini Mouse at close to Mach 4—not that "Mach" meant much of anything in the moon's almost non-existent atmosphere, but it was a convenient term to use to measure velocity—at two thousand meters altitude. When the target came in sight they'd have sixty-three seconds to the fire-and-climb point; sixty-three seconds to lock onto the target and blast it. Nobody, of course, knew what—if any—defenses the launch sites had. But those defenses, if they existed, would have very little time to realize they were under attack, aim, and fire. Unless they had an early warning system, in which case they'd be ready before the Piranhas crossed the visual horizon. If they had an early warning system, Piranha squadron would have to go to Plan B—and would surely have losses.

Mini Mouse had begun life as a dwarf planet, captured by Troy during the system's early childhood. As such it had an iron core, unlike Dumbo, Troy's other moon, that had been torn from the planet's crust during system formation. Even though it was smaller than Earth's moon, the iron core gave Mini Mouse a slightly higher gravity, about .2 G. The gravity aided the *Scott*'s squadrons in approaching their targets from below the horizon. Despite possible problems, the approach looked like it was going to be a milk run.

Then the first division was visible over the target's horizon.

VSFA 132, "Piranha" Squadron, Approaching Target

Defensive weapons, similar to the Beanbags used by the NAUS for missile defense, began throwing up a wall of tiny pellets for the Kestrels to run into. But by the time they did, the range-to-target was so short, and the Kestrels' velocities so great, that the munitions didn't have enough time to fully deploy before the attacking craft were past them. Other weapons opened up, rapidly firing off slugs that could pulverize a fighter if one ran into enough of them. Again, the First division was too close, and the slugs missed, allowing all four Kestrels to fire their munitions, some of which knocked out some of the defensive weapons.

But the other three divisions were ten, twenty, and thirty seconds behind, and the surviving alien defenses were now alerted.

"Big Mouth, Piranha Seven, something hit me!" That was Ensign Charles H. Hammann, the third pilot in the Second division.

Street's display showed Hammann's fighter craft climbing, but flashing red in a sequence that told her that it was not only damaged but out of its carefully calculated arabesque as well.

Another icon began flashing red and stopped moving. It was Piranha 14, piloted by Third division's Ensign Daniel Sullivan. It was down, and Street wasn't receiving vitals—that indicated that Sullivan was likely dead.

Two icons from division Four turned red, but Street didn't bother checking to see who they were, she was too busy doing a damage assessment of the target.

The defensive weapons had ceased fire. Street had no way of knowing whether that was because they were all destroyed, because they were out of munitions, or because the weapons couldn't fire that close to vertical. As seen in the view from her tail camera, even with the clouds of debris from division Four's Scatter Blasts still expanding, the target area looked like it was thoroughly chewed up. There was no satellite image to check against.

It didn't matter either way; VSFA 132 didn't have any Scatter-Blasts for a second run.

"Nibblers, Nibblers, all Nibblers, this is Big Teeth," Street said into her squadron circuit. "We've done all we can for now. Let's head for home." She cleared her throat before adding, "Downed Nibblers, hang in there. Rescue will be on its way as soon as possible. Maybe they're on their way even now. I've noted and sent in your positions, so SAR will be able to head for your location even before they have a lock on you. Big Teeth out."

She checked Piranha Seven's icon. It still displayed a wobbly path, but the Kestrel was still rising, and was keeping up with the rest of the squadron. Her squadron still had three Kestrels down and out of communication; she didn't know if the pilots were alive and well—except for Piranha Seven, whose lack of vitals indicated he was dead—or if they were in imminent danger of being captured.

Command Center; 1st Marine Combat Force,
Outside Millerton

"Admiral," Lieutenant General Harold Bauer said to the image on his comm once Avery had described the situation and said what he wanted from the Marines, "you get your SAR craft to me and I'll give you the security you need."

"Your assistance is greatly appreciated, General." Rear Admiral Avery's reply came seconds later. He was in his CAC on board the *Durango* in orbit. "Just remember, the SAR Pegasus craft can't carry a large force."

"I'm well aware of the space limitations of the Pegasus. One squad should be more than adequate for each mission, and won't overly tax the crafts' systems."

"Give me the coordinates of the platoon you're assigning to the mission, I'll have the Pegasuses land at its location."

Bauer shook his head. "I'm not assigning one platoon to the mission, but one squad from each regiment.

Avery arched an eyebrow at that. "Are you trying to prevent one platoon from absorbing too many casualties?"

"I'd rather say I'm spreading the experience throughout my division." Bauer even almost believed what he said.

India Company, Fifteen Kilometers East of Millerton

3rd Battalion had stopped on a rough line some distance east of Millerton, in an area that on Earth would be called a scrub forest; widely spaced trees that looked stunted, and thin undergrowth. The plain was scoured flat except for the boulders, some sitting higher than a human, some small enough for someone unobservant to trip over, and every size in between, that dotted the plain. The extensive boulder field gave clear evidence that Troy had suffered through at least one ice age; the boulders looked like they'd been carried here by ice sheets from distant locations and dropped in place when the glaciers withdrew. The Marines settled behind boulders and thicker tree trunks. None of them bothered to dig a fighting hole, or even scrape a shallow hollow to lie in. They waited for word of what to do next. When it came, it wasn't anything they expected.

"First squad, on me," Staff Sergeant Guillen shouted.

Lance Corporal Mackie looked around from his position on the platoon's defensive line and saw the platoon sergeant standing erect about twenty meters behind the position. He gave a quick glance to his front, then at Adriance, who was already rising to his feet.

"Move it, people!" Sergeant Martin shouted.

"First fire team, up and at 'em," Corporal Adriance ordered.

Mackie stood and reached for his pack.

"Weapons only, leave your packs in place," Guillen shouted. "Get over here now!"

In less than a minute, the thirteen Marines of the squad were gathered in a semi-circle in front of the platoon sergeant. Second Lieutenant Commiskey joined him.

"By now you've probably heard about the missile strike on ARG17. They came from launch sites on Mini Mouse." Commiskey paused for a few seconds while some of the Marines snickered at the small moon's name. "The carrier *Scott* launched four squadrons to kill those launch sites before they could fire more missiles. The sites had defensive systems, and knocked down some of the Kestrels.

"There are Navy pilots on the surface of Mini Mouse. Some of them might still be alive. At the request of Rear Admiral Avery, Lieutenant General Bauer has tasked the 1st Marines with providing a squad as security for one of the Navy search and rescue teams going in to retrieve the downed pilots. You're the squad."

Mackie blinked at "retrieve." You *rescue* live people, but you *retrieve* corpses.

He must not have been the only one who reacted to the word, because Commiskey quickly added, "'Retrieve' is the word the Admiral used. But as far as anybody knows, most—maybe all—of the downed pilots are still alive. Four squadrons attacked the launch sites, all four had losses. One squad from each regiment and one from the division recon company will go with the SAR craft on the rescue mission. Third platoon has been chosen as the 1st Marines' SAR team. We don't know what kind of ground defenses the enemy has for the sites, so we'll essentially be going in blind. For this mission, we'll be in armored vacuum suits."

He paused for a moment before saying, "Remember, that even though armored vacuum suits give protection from all small arms in the NAUS arsenal, fragments from conventional explosive munitions, and limited protection from both stellar radiation and weapon radiation, they aren't impervious to everything. We don't know what kind of weapons the enemy will throw at us, or if they even have defenses against ground forces. Mini Mouse has an atmosphere so thin it's virtually a hard vacuum. So whatever else you do, don't let your suit get punctured.

"That is all. Staff Sergeant Guillen will take over now. Staff Sergeant, the platoon is yours."

"Yes, sir." Guillen briefly came to attention, but didn't salute. They were in presumably hostile territory. A salute could attract sniper fire if any enemy were in the area, so Marines didn't salute in the field.

Guillen watched Commiskey head toward the jumble of boulders where Captain Sitter had established the company headquarters, then turned to the men.

"When I dismiss you, return to your positions and resume your watch. When the word comes down, I'll take the squad leaders to get the armored vacuum suits from supply. Any questions? Yes, Zion."

"Ah, Staff Sergeant, when we go, is anybody going to relieve us here?" PFC Zion gave a nervous look over his shoulder at the ground the platoon hadn't secured.

Guillen curled his lip before answering. "Zion, that's above your pay grade to worry about. But, yes, somebody will relieve us in this position. Don't ask who. 'Who' is above *my* pay grade."

He looked from Marine to Marine with an expression that asked, *Does anybody else have a dumb question?* but nobody else seemed anxious to ask anything. "If there are no other questions, Sergeant Martin, get your people back in position and wait for further orders. Dismissed."

Leaning close as they started back toward their positions, Adriance murmured, "Stand by for a head smack, Zion."

"In stereo," Mackie added from Zion's other side.

"What'd I do?" Zion demanded indignantly.

"That's two," said PFC Orndoff.

"Two what? And how come you're all ganging up on me?"

"Dumb questions, peon," Adriance said. "And that makes three. Keep it up, and I'll have to let Orndoff give you a head smack, too, because head-smacking you will be more than a two-man job."

Then they were back at their position. Adriance sat with his back against a tree trunk. Mackie stayed on his feet, leaning over a chest high boulder. Orndoff climbed a tree, and Zion went prone next to a waist high boulder. They appeared relaxed and casual—to anyone who could make them out in their camouflage utilities—but appearances were deceptive. Their eyes were in constant motion, alertly search-ing the landscape to their front, checking their sides. Every few minutes Adriance slid his infrared viewer into place before his eyes to search for warm bodies that might not be noticed in visual light. And Mackie frequently checked the fire team's motion detector, looking for movement that wasn't vegetation shifting in the moving air—and was bigger than a mid-sized dog.

So situated, they quietly, alertly, waited for an hour. Then the word came: "Chow down. We go in thirty."

En Route to Mini Mouse

A Navy chief petty officer met the Marines when the McKinzie elevator reached geosync; a squad from the 6th Marines, one from the 7th, and another from 1st Recon filled out the rescue security teams. The CPO was slender, dressed in greasy khakis, and had a headset perched behind his ears. Something that looked suspiciously like a half-smoked cigar but couldn't possibly be—it couldn't *really* be a cigar, could it?—stuck out of the corner of his mouth.

"Ah right, ever'body here?" he drawled. The question must have been rhetorical because he didn't wait for an answer. "I'm Chief Petty Officer Othniel Tripp, and I'm in charge of this here boardin' station. Squadron VSFA 132 lost four fighter craft on their bombing run on one of the alien launch sites. We've got four Pegasus birds—that's what we call our search an' rescue birds, Pegasuses, after the flyin' horses in the Grik stories—going in after 'em. Youse going along to protect the crews in case the aliens have infantry there what needs to be fought off. Our Pegasus crews are better'n anybody else's at searchin' and rescuin', but they ain't so great at rifle fightin'. That's why you're going along. I got four birds out here, you got four squads. That works out jes perfect, one squad one bird. That's a lot better'n four squads an' one bird. You're gonna be pretty cramped as is in them suits youse wearin'."

The Marines were very bulky in the armored vacuum suits that had been waiting for them at the foot of McKinzie —it turned out that they hadn't been delivered to India Company's supply sergeant. The armor's weight—armor, no matter how light, is always heavy—was offset by servos in the main joints that not only allowed the Marines to move as easily as they would unarmored, but added to their strength.

"When your bird lands, the flight commander will tell you if he wants you outside or to stay in. If he tells you outside, be ready to fight right off. Now, you outta know, the flight commander is an officer, the pilot is a first class, the crew chief is a third class, and the—."

Tripp suddenly looked away from the Marines, pulled his headset's earpieces forward and rotated the mike to his mouth. He listened for a moment, murmured a reply, then looked back up.

"Ah right, who's first? Pegasus One is docked and waiting for you." His drawl disappeared and he became all business. He stepped to the airlock's hatch, which was closed.

"First Marines, that's you. Come with me." Chief Tripp led them to the entrance to the docking chute.

"Line up by fire teams," Sergeant Martin ordered his squad, and took a position on the other side of the airlock from the chief.

Corporal Adriance stood between them facing the hatch. Lance Corporal Mackie took position behind him, and glanced back to make sure PFCs Orndoff and Zion were in place.

"We're ready, Chief," Martin told Tripp as soon as the squad was in line.

Tripp tapped a three touch code on the hatch's lock, and it slid aside. "Go!" he barked. Adriance stepped forward, and the rest of the squad followed. Martin brought up the rear.

Inside the Pegasus a crewman, anonymous in a vacuum suit with a reflective faceplate, directed the Marines to narrow benches along the sides of the cabin.

"No space between you," he said. "We're so tight some of you might have to sit on the deck. Close it up and keep it close!"

Mackie reflexively shook his head when he saw the interior of the cabin. It looked barely big enough to hold an armored vacuum suited fire team, much less an entire squad. "Are we really going to be sitting on each other's laps?" he asked nobody in particular, then when nobody answered: "That's what I thought."

The Marines jammed themselves in. Six squeezed onto the bench along each side. They weren't able to sit straight with their backs against the bulkhead, but twisted their torsos so they overlapped, one man's shoulder in front of the next one's. There was little space between their knees and the knees of the Marines on the opposite side. Martin and Private Frank Hill, the squad's newest and most junior man, managed to find space on the floor amid the feet and knees.

"Hold on, we're about to move," the anonymous crewman alerted them from his station, which was out of sight from the main cabin. "Hold on tight so you don't get banged around."

"Hold onto what?" Orndoff muttered over the fire team circuit.

"Your ass, that's what," Mackie answered.

Adriance snorted, then ordered, "Shitcan the grabass, people. This is serious."

But Orndoff was right; there wasn't anything to grab hold of.

The search and rescue craft lurched, separating from the elevator airlock, throwing the Marines against each other. But they were already tight enough that nobody built enough momentum to injure himself or the Marine he bumped into. Slow acceleration eased Pegasus One away from the geosync station. There were no ports to look through, no display panels to show what was outside; no way to tell where they were, what direction they were headed, how fast they were going, how much time was passing. All the Marines could do was wait, with greater or lesser degrees of patience.

After an indeterminate length of time the anonymous crewman announced from his unseen station, "Halfway there."

Wherever *there* was, and however far *halfway* might be.

Eventually a different voice came to the Marines. "We're going down," the voice—the flight commander?—said. "When we hit, the rear hatch will drop, and I need you to get out there instantly. It looks like bad guys are closing on Piranha 14's position."

When the voice—the pilot? the SAR commander?—didn't say anything more, Sergeant Martin demanded, "How many of them are there? What direction are they coming from? Do they have armor or are they on foot or what? Come on, man, we need more data or we're stepping into an ambush!"

"No time!" the voice said. "We're down." There was a jolt of impact as the Pegasus hit the ground. The hatch in the compartment's rear dropped and became a ramp.

The major joints of the armored vacuum suits had servo motors, made necessary by the mass of the suits. The Marines had been sitting in cramped positions without being able to move. Third platoon's First squad looked clumsy scrambling down the ramp, but without the servos, they couldn't have even stood to shamble off until full circulation returned to their limbs.

"Where are they?" Sergeant Martin demanded as he looked around in attempt to find the foe.

"I'm sending you our feed now," the unidentified voice said.

Martin put it on his HUD for a quick study, and swore. He began shouting orders.

Mini Mouse, LZ 1

"First fire team, get to that Kestrel!" Sergeant Martin shouted. "Second and Third, lay down fire on those vehicles!"

The downed Kestrel was a hundred meters away to the northeast. To the north-northeast, two vehicles of an alien design were bouncing toward them at a high rate of speed from less than two kilometers away.

"First fire team, let's go!" Corporal Adriance shouted, and began the shuffling low-gravity walk men had used since Neil Armstrong first stepped on Earth's moon centuries earlier.

Three crewmen from the Pegasus were already on their way, driving a motorized litter to carry the pilot back.

Second and Third fire teams began firing on the approaching vehicles. The Marines' rifles were loaded with alternating armor piercing and explosive rounds. The armor piercing bullets bounced off the armored fronts of the vehicles, the explosive ones barely pitted the surface. The enemy didn't give immediate return fire; maybe they didn't have a mechanism that would compensate for the bouncing.

First fire team reached the Kestrel just as the rescue men were loading the unmoving pilot onto the litter; the Marines couldn't tell if he was conscious or not, or even if he was still alive.

Adriance saw how ineffective the fire from the rest of the squad was, and knew that adding fire from four more rifles on their fronts wouldn't do anything to stop the alien vehicles. He decided to do something else.

"First fire team, try to ricochet your rounds to the undercarriage of the one on the left," he ordered, and began firing into the regolith in front of the vehicle, sending fragments of stone bouncing into its lower front and underneath it. In an instant, the other three Marines began firing the same.

"Our armored vehicles have their strongest armor on their fronts," Adriance explained absently as he maintained steady fire, "and the weakest on the bottom. If these bad guys build theirs the same way, we might be able to break through."

Maybe, maybe not, but it was worth a try—and it was. Something broke in the vehicle. Gases began venting from its bottom. It slewed to a stop, turning its side to the Marines. The vehicle on the right had to swerve violently to its left to avoid running into its damaged mate, throwing up a curtain of dust and gravel before pointing back toward the humans.

Sergeant Martin saw what First fire team did. "Second and Third fire teams," he shouted, "did you see what they did? Do the same thing—bounce your rounds underneath the one that's still coming at us."

By then, the occupants of the first vehicle, a dozen of them, had scrambled out of it and were charging in high, jinking bounds at the Marines by the Kestrel. The shape of their vacuum suits would have stunned the Marines had they not already seen the vids and stills brought back by Force Recon, and sent during the original alien attack on Troy. The legs were long, and bent the wrong way; the arms were too short; forward-jutting heads stuck out on very long necks. A large bulge on the rear of the suits counter-balanced the heads. They ran bent at the hips almost parallel to the ground.

The charging aliens were firing rifles, but their shots were wild and none seemed to come near the Marines. They were closing fast, their run was much faster than the Marines' shuffle, but they didn't seem to be as well trained at low gravity movement. Or maybe their jinking wasn't suitable for rapid movement in low gravity. They kept stumbling and tripping.

The Marines of First fire team took advantage of the stumbles and trips to take aim during the brief seconds their targets were relatively motionless. The armor piercing bullets mostly glanced off the aliens' armor, but some of the explosive bullets punctured them, venting air.

"First fire team, get back here," Martin ordered when the litter was halfway back to the Pegasus.

"Let's go!" Adriance repeated the order to his men. He looked to see that they were obeying. "That includes you, Zion."

But Zion didn't move; he was half sitting, folded over his rifle.

Adriance swore. "Mackie, check Zion!"

Mackie had already began the shuffle-run back to the Pegasus and had to turn back. Adriance didn't wait for him, he was already kneeling over Zion when Mackie reached him.

Adriance's face was barely visible through his faceplate when he looked at Mackie, but his expression was grim. Not all of the aliens' shots had gone wild.

"Marines don't leave their dead," the fire team leader said, thick-voiced. "Give me a hand."

When the two of them raised Zion, Mackie saw where a hole had been punched through the neck of the other's armor where it was jointed to his chest plate. Air had vented explosively, blowing the hole much larger. Blood had vented as well from a wound in Zion's throat, staining the edges of the hole red. They draped his arms over their shoulders and ran, with Adriance carrying Zion's rifle.

By then, fire from the rest of the squad had crippled the second vehicle, and the Marines were firing at the bounding, jinking, stumbling aliens. Only a dozen were still making the mad charge. But not all of the dozen who were down had been hit; at least four of them had gone prone to give aimed return fire.

"Let's move it, First fire team!" Martin shouted. "This bird is almost ready to fly away. The squids'll leave you if you aren't here when they're ready to go!" He looked at the prone aliens giving return fire, and ordered, "Second fire team, take him out." He fired a shot himself at one of the shooters to show who he meant. In seconds, four more bullets struck that one, and he stopped shooting.

"Now get the other shooters!"

The lead running aliens reached the Pegasus at the same time as Adriance and Mackie, and one of them barreled into the two of them and their burden, knocking them down.

Mackie kicked out as he fell, smashing an armored foot into the alien's backward-bending knee, felling him. The Marine jumped up and stomped on the alien's helmet, then grasped his rifle with one hand behind the receiver and the other in the middle of the forestock. He saw another alien rushing at him with his weapon pointed like a spear. Mackie pirouetted out of the way of the lunge, and slammed the butt of his rifle at his assailant's head. But the momentum of his spin carried him around and off balance, so his blow barely staggered the alien. But that slight stagger was enough to allow Adriance to swing his rifle around in a wicked blow that shattered the alien's facemask.

With two down at their feet, Mackie and Adriance had a few seconds to take in the entire fight. It was one-on-one, man-to-man close combat—man to alien; they had to be aliens, there was no way a human being could jam into one of their vacuum suits without breaking bones and disjointing limbs.

No one was shooting in the melee; the combatants faced too much danger of hitting their own if they did. They were all using their weapons as clubs, quarterstaffs, or thrusting spears.

Just a couple of meters away, Orndoff was being forced backward by an alien jabbing and thrusting at him. Mackie and Adriance both stepped toward the two. Adriance swung the butt of his rifle in a golf club stroke at the alien's low-slung head while Mackie reversed his weapon and slammed its butt into the alien's side. Orndoff's attacker fell away in an uncontrolled tumble, and came to rest twisted in ways that couldn't be natural for its kind.

Corporal Button, the Third fire team leader, went down clutching his abdomen. The alien who had knocked him down jumped on his helmet, but in the low gravity lacked the force necessary to break anything. Button rolled away but wasn't able to regain his feet as the alien pursued him with repeated, rapid kicks. Adriance leaped in Button's direction to help him.

Mackie shuffled to the aid of Second fire team's PFC Harry Harvey, who was closer and parrying off rapid blows from another alien.

Orndoff screamed a war cry, heard only by the Marines through their helmet comms. He leaped at the back of one of two aliens attacking Lance Corporal Fernando L. Garcia. He misjudged in the low gravity and sailed over the alien, but managed to slam his rifle's butt downward onto the alien's neck, jarring him. The alien whipped his head around to see what had hit him and saw Orndoff, off balance from hitting him, thud onto the regolith and tumble. The alien leaped at the Marine, freeing Garcia to concentrate on his other attacker.

Orndoff twisted to turn his tumble into a controlled roll, so he was facing up when the alien pounced at him. The alien's jump was better than Orndoff's had been, but he still flew high and came down slowly in the low gravity. The Marine had time to twist his body to the side to miss the worst of the alien's jump, and brace himself to lunge upward with his rifle. The alien already realized that swinging his rifle club-like would throw him off balance; he came down with his rifle pointed straight down, to spear his opponent. He missed Orndoff's twisting body, but the Marine connected with his target when he lunged up and plunged the muzzle of his rifle into the joint where the elongated helmet met the top plate of the neck armor. The alien's limbs shot out away from its body, then it jerked its hands to its throat and clutched at Orndoff's rifle barrel. He crashed onto his side, yanking the rifle out of the Marine's grip. Orndoff jumped to his feet and tried to retrieve his rifle, but it was jammed too tightly into the alien's armor.

Orndoff spun around in a hands-extended crouch, ready to grab or parry any weapon coming at him. The closest alien he saw was the second one attacking Garcia. Garcia had that alien down and was slamming the butt of his rifle repeatedly into his helmet.

A few meters beyond, Mackie had also lost his rifle. He ducked past a thrust from an alien and grabbed its neck just behind its head. Bracing himself, Mackie twisted, spinning around and flinging the alien's body off the ground like a whip. Halfway through a twirl, he fell backward, but didn't release the alien's neck. The alien thudded to the ground and sprawled limply. Mackie hopped upward and kicked the alien's head. It flopped at the end of its long neck. He looked around and saw Adriance down with an alien grabbing at his facemask, looking like it was prying it open. Mackie dove at the alien, hitting him full force on his side. The alien bounced along the ground almost like a flat rock skipping across a pond. Mackie raced after it to grab its neck before it could recover, and fling it the same way he'd killed the other one.

This alien was faster, and was on his feet facing Mackie before the Marine reached him. The two, both without rifles, crashed together. The human was heavier than the alien, and drove him back. The alien flipped, so his head was toward Mackie's feet. Unable to grab the alien's neck the way he had the other one, Mackie wrapped his arms around his torso and stood erect, squeezing as tightly as his augmented arm strength could. It wasn't enough to crush the armor, or even dent it.

The alien struggled, but his arms were too short to wrap around Mackie's legs to pull him off his feet. His legs, though, were big and powerful. He kicked them wildly, and threw Mackie off balance. They crashed on their sides to the regolith. The alien slammed his head against Mackie's legs, and Mackie kicked back at his neck and the underside of his head before letting go and rolling away and bounding up into a crouch.

The alien was already up and leaping at the Marine. Mackie threw himself backward and thrust out with his feet, catching the alien on the upper part of his chest. The alien's momentum rolled Mackie into a reverse somersault, and the Marine's legs were a lever that threw the alien over him and away.

This time Mackie was on his feet first, and reached the alien in time to grab its upper neck. He jerked upward, lifting the alien off the ground, and slammed him onto the regolith hard enough to make him bounce. He grabbed the alien's neck with his hands almost half a meter apart, and brought it down sharply across his knee. He thought he felt something break inside the armor. The alien went into uncontrollable spasms. Mackie gave its head an extra kick, and looked around for another alien.

The fight was ending. Eight Marines and no aliens were standing.

"Fire team leaders, report!" Sergeant Martin's voice was hoarse over the comm.

"I'm here," Mackie reported. "Adriance?" he asked when his fire team leader didn't reply. Instantly, he took over. "Orndoff, are you all right?"

"I'm five by," Orndoff answered, breathing heavily. "Where's Adriance?"

The fire team leaders' reports took longer than they should have because both Corporals Adriance and Button were down. So was Third fire team's PFC Hermann Kuchneister. PFCs Zion and David Porter were both dead.

Corpsmen from the Pegasus were checking the wounded before the fire team leaders' report was finished.

"All right, Marines, get everybody loaded," a voice—the pilot? the SAR commander?—ordered. "Leave the aliens, we don't have room to take any of them. Maybe we can come back later to deal with them."

Two minutes later, the Pegasus took off with a short rolling start. The two dead were propped in corners, the wounded laid out on the deck between the benches.

The Aftermath of the Mini Mouse Missions

In retrospect, it was a good thing that the squads assigned to security duty for the Pegasuses on the Search and Rescue missions were from different regiments. Three of the four squads had contact on the ground, and all three of those suffered casualties. India Company's squad hadn't suffered the most, nor had it suffered the least. Among them, the four squads lost a total of five Marines, with ten more wounded. Most of the latter were expected to recover and return to duty. That would have been very heavy losses for one platoon; forty percent of its strength.

All of the aliens who fought the Marines were killed.

This was the first combat experience for most of the Marines involved, the first time they'd had to kill in order to live, the first time they'd had to deal with buddies getting wounded or killed.

And they still didn't have a clue who these aliens were who they'd had to kill, or why those aliens attacked had Troy and the fleet.

With the operation on Mini Mouse underway, Rear Admiral Avery turned his attention back to Amphibious Ready Group 17. The attack was over, all the enemy missiles had been destroyed by the squadrons sent after them, or by fire from the warships—or they'd hit their targets. The wormhole had closed before more than two of the drones he'd sent made it through; all they'd tell Earth was that a missile attack on ARG17 was under way.

Too many alien missiles had made it through the defenses to their targets.

A debris cloud marked where the Amphibious Assault Ship *Peleliu*, ARG 17's flagship, had been. Likewise the AAS *Kandahar* and *Juno Beach*. A single cloud marked the death site of the Landing Platform Shuttle *Phillips Head* and the Logistics Supply Ship *Richmond*. Another showed where the Amphibious Landing Ferry *Yorktown* had been destroyed. The Dry Cargo Ship *Columbus* was dead.

The Amphibious Assault Ships *Grandar Bay*, and *Fallujah* were wounded, as were the Landing Platform Shuttle *Iwo Jima* and the Amphibious Landing Dock *Saratoga*. The DCS *Amundsen* was wounded.

Three other ships of ARG17 were dead; only four of the nineteen had made it through without serious injury.

Task Force 8 had also suffered severely. Four of the five warships Avery had sent to meet and escort ARG17 to Troy from the wormhole were gone. The destroyers *Lance Corporal Keith Lopez* and *Chief Gunners Mate Oscar Schmit Jr.* were dead, and both of TF8's cruisers, the *Coral Sea* and the *Ramsey Strait*. Only the fast attack carrier *Rear Admiral Isaac C. Kidd* survived, and she was severely damaged. Damaged or not, she was trying to recover those of her Meteors that had survived the fight with the alien missiles.

Avery spent a long time looking at the results of the enemy attack on the ARG. Fourteen of the nineteen starships in the ARG were troop transports. Six of the fourteen were dead, probably lost with all hands. Five of the others were damaged, with an as yet unknown number of casualties. Only three had come through without significant battle damage or casualties. Three of the five support ships were dead, and one other was wounded.

Perhaps the worst loss was that of the *Peleliu* with the ARG's admiral, and the commanding general of VII Corps and his primary staff.

Finally Avery said in a formal voice, "Comm, get me commander, Marine Combat Force, Troy."

"Aye aye, sir," Lieutenant Commander Davis said softly; he'd been following the aftermath of ARG17's encounter with the missiles along with the admiral.

While waiting for the Marine commander, Avery called to his aide, Lieutenant Julius Townsend. "Kindly arrange for my transportation planetside, to Lieutenant General Bauer's headquarters." He hesitated, then added, "Tell Chief Jones I want to take the fast way down."

"Aye aye, sir." Townsend, understanding why his boss needed to meet with Bauer in person and as soon as possible, put a call in to Chief Boatswain's Mate Andrew Jones, who ran the admiral's ship-to-ship, orbit-to-ground shuttles, and told him to be ready to take off on either at a moment's notice. "The Admiral wants to fly down fastest."

"No problem, Lieutenant. My bird will be ready by the time the admiral gets here. Even if he starts right now."

"Thanks, Chief." To Avery: "Chief Jones says he's ready, sir."

"Thank you, Mr. Townsend. Comm, belay that last. Inform Lieutenant General Bauer I am en route to his location and will provide him with an ETA shortly."

Near the McKinzie Elevator Base,
Outside Millerton, Marine Headquarters

"Admiral," Lieutenant General Bauer said, rising and stepping from behind his small field desk. "Come in, please. Have a seat." He gestured at two camp chairs sitting at a small folding table. A coffee set-up was already on the table.

"Thank you, sir," Avery replied. He nervously stepped to one of the camp chairs but didn't sit; Bauer out-ranked him, and protocol said the senior man sits first. That's what he told himself.

"Don't stand on ceremony, Jim," Bauer said, smiling. "We're in the field, not the Flag Club. When a man wearing more stars than you tells you to have a seat, you sit your ass down."

"Whatever you say, Harry." Avery plopped into the chair facing into the room. He fidgeted.

"Rough ride down?" Bauer asked as he sat in the other camp chair.

Avery nodded. "'Fast ride on a rocky road,' as you Marines call that plunge." He grimaced, than picked up his coffee mug and took a sip. "I thought I should get down here ASAP." He shook his head. "The way my arthritic joints feel, maybe I should have ridden the elevator instead of taking the shuttle all the way."

Bauer snorted. "Arthritic my ass. There's a lot of negative things that a Marine can say about the Navy—some of them are even true—but complaints about medical care aren't among them. If you have arthritis, it's because you want it."

Avery chuckled. "Yeah. Maybe it's just age getting to me." He looked into a corner of Bauer's Spartan office. "Or maybe it's thinking about our losses."

Bauer sucked in a deep breath. "Tell me all about it. Starting with why you thought it important to pay me a personal visit rather than use your comms when you should be in your CAC directing rescue and recover operations on ARG 17."

Avery flinched at the mild criticism. "It's serious, Harry. Damn serious. I don't want any bad guys who might be listening in to hear me say just how bad things suddenly got."

"I can buy that." Bauer glanced at a random part of the ceiling. "That was quite a light show we were treated to shortly before you announced your impending visit. What the hell happened up there?"

Avery looked at Bauer, and his expression was bleak. "I lost a third of my fighting power. Ships and men. Gone. Dead." He shuddered. "But that's not the worst of it. VII Corps basically no longer exists. ARG 17 got slaughtered, despite the best efforts of my people. We just weren't prepared for an attack like that." He shook his head, and shuddered again. "Two of VII Corps' divisions are gone completely— unless some of the troops managed to get into stasis. If any did, it wasn't many; there weren't enough stasis stations on the ships to handle that many people. One of the other two divisions was hurt so badly I don't think it can function as a division again until it's withdrawn and reconstituted." He stopped talking and looked into a place that only he could see.

"I must be relieved of command, I don't deserve command," Avery said so softly the Marine barely heard him, then was silent again.

After a moment of waiting for him to say more, Bauer asked, "What about the Fourth division? What about General Lyman and his staff?"

Avery shook himself, then spoke more firmly and briskly than he had before. "I believe the 25th Infantry Division lost half a brigade but is otherwise intact." He paused again, swallowed, and continued in a firm voice. "General Lyman and his staff, unfortunately, were on the *Peleliu* when she was killed. I don't believe there were any survivors."

Bauer stared at Avery. What he had just described had to be the worst military disaster in centuries.

He didn't say that, though. Instead he asked, "Have you sent word back to Earth yet?"

Avery shook his head. "I wanted to make sure you assumed command before I send word."

"Jim, if what you said about Lyman being killed is accurate, I'm now the senior officer on or near Troy. Of course I'm in command." Bauer switched to another topic.

"I lost some Marines in the rescue mission to Mini Mouse. What is the Navy's assessment of the lunar operations?"

Now on firmer ground, not thinking directly about his lost ships and sailors, Avery calmed down. "I'm sorry about your Marines, but the mission was a success on multiple levels. First, they brought back all of my downed fliers. Second, the enemy didn't use any defensive fire. Did you know I had drones out there to mimic attacking spacecraft, to attract fire? Well, I did, and the enemy didn't fire on them. The drones over-flew all four sites to assess damage. It didn't look like anything could have survived in the bombed areas."

"Then where did those ground counter-attacks come from?"

Avery shook his head apologetically. "The drones didn't see anything that might have been their bases." He shrugged. "But they weren't looking for them, either."

"Those bases, if they exist, need to be found and neutralized," Bauer said firmly.

"Agreed." Avery bobbed his head, and mentally kicked himself for not ordering a search for ground bases on Mini Mouse before he headed planetside. "I'll order a search as soon as we are through here."

"What is your assessment of the survivability of the people on the starships that were killed?"

"I'm sure some are still alive, in compartments that weren't breached. More than that I can't say at this time. Crews from the uninjured ships are conducting searches. I won't know until I get their reports. The surviving Meteors off the *Kidd* are searching the damaged and killed Meteors for surviving pilots." His shoulders jerked in a half-shrug. "The Meteors' cockpits are survival capsules. If they didn't get holed, the pilots can last up to twelve hours before their life support starts to fail." He looked again into a dark corner of his mind and murmured, "Some of them might still make it back alive."

"Admiral Avery!" Bauer said sharply. "Time enough for that later. Right now we need to rescue everybody who can be rescued and recover those who can't. We need to fully assess the damage to our forces, and prepare to fend off the next alien attack. There *will* be another attack."

Avery flinched as though slapped, but pulled himself out of the depression he'd been sinking into. "You're right, General. You're in command, what are your orders?"

"All you have left for planet defense is your flagship, the big carrier, and three frigates. Is that right?"

"Yes."

"What about the two destroyers you had pursuing the missiles?"

"They are still en route to what remains of ARG 17."

"Good. They can aid in the search and recovery."

"Yes they can."

"Next, you have inter-stel comms, I don't. So I need for you to send a preliminary report to the Joint Chiefs."

"I will pass my message by you before transmission."

Bauer waved that away. "I trust your judgment, and you're better able than I am to tell the Chiefs the status of the Navy forces here, and request what you need. Tell them to start feeding Second Army here."

Avery nodded his acceptance of Bauer's instruction.

"And I want you to find the aliens' ground bases on Mini Mouse. Also, commence satellite reconnaissance of Dumbo. If the aliens had bases on the smaller moon, they probably have installations of some sort on the larger one as well."

"I'll give the orders as soon as I leave your command post."

"Excellent!" Bauer exclaimed, rising to his feet. "Can you think of anything else that needs to be done at this time?"

"No, sir. I think we covered everything."

"Good. Keep me up to date on what's happening with the search and recovery operations, and what you're finding on the moons."

"Aye aye, General."

Bauer held out his hand, and was relieved at the firmness of Avery's grip. If Avery's grip had been weak, Bauer would have relieved him of command and passed it to the senior surviving captain in either fleet.

Now to prepare his Marines for the next ground attack by the aliens. One thing that wasn't mentioned in his meeting with Avery, but that Bauer knew full well: the engagement on Mini Mouse demonstrated that, in close combat, his Marines were the superior fighters, and they could beat greater numbers.

Remembering the vids he'd seen of the original attack on Troy, and the little from Force Recon, Bauer knew it would be a very tough fight when it came. It would be a fight that might well be decided by numbers.

Unknown was how many soldiers of VII Corps survived the attack on ARG 17, and the state of their morale. High morale and belief in yourself and your comrades was of incalculable value in battle. They were what doctrine and field manuals called "force magnifiers," the intangibles that increased a military unit's ability to fight and win without increasing its size or weapons.

"Sir." A firm knock came on the frame of Bauer's office door. He looked toward it and saw Lieutenant Upshur.

"Come."

Upshur stepped inside the room. "Sir, satellite observation reports a wormhole opening twenty degrees above ecleptic, one point starboard of galactic east. Half a light minute distance."

Galactic east was almost opposite the direction to Earth, and no other human colonized worlds were in that direction.

Damn Navy. Why do they have to use "points" to give direction? Bauer thought but didn't say. He, like most Marines—and just about everybody else for that matter—had to translate points to degrees. A compass point was one thirty-second of a compass rose, slightly more than five and a half degrees. It was good that this wormhole was only one point off galactic east; figuring seven points would have taken more time.

Bauer waited for more.

"So far, nothing has exited the wormhole," Upshur said.

"I need to know instantly when something does."

"Yes, sir. I will inform you immediately when something exits."

"And get me Brigadier General Porter, ASAP."

"Aye aye, sir!" Upshur wasn't at all surprised by the "ASAP" rather than the more common, "At his earliest convenience." The just-opened wormhole could only mean the aliens were about to make an appearance.

Less than a minute had passed since Bauer told Upshur he wanted his chief of staff, and the man was already there.

"You must have been waiting for my call."

"As soon as I heard about the wormhole, I knew you'd need me."

"You found out about it before I did? Upshur is *my* aide, he should report to me first."

Porter shook his head. "He didn't tell me. I was in the comm shack when the message came in from orbit."

"Where do we need to aim to hit a target one point to starboard of galactic east?"

Porter shrugged. "Sometimes it seems the Navy thinks they're still at sea in wooden ships with canvas sails."

Bauer grunted. "Well, defending against starships coming from one point to starboard is going to be their job. We have to defend the ground from both land and air attack. Assemble the staff."

"Aye aye, sir."

Briefing room, 1st Marine Combat Force Headquarters,
Near Millerton

Word of the new wormhole traveled fast, and it was only minutes before every member of the 1st Marine Combat Force's primary staff and their seconds were assembled, along with the commanders of all the major subordinate units.

"Gentlemen," Bauer began, "we don't know when the aliens are going to exit the wormhole or in what force. What we do know is, when they do come we can expect a most serious fight. Using only missiles launched from Mini Mouse, they killed or severely injured three quarters of ARG 17, and a third of TF 8. Along with the ships of ARG 17, the aliens killed or damaged more than half of VII Corps before those poor soldiers could even see the world they were on their way to. The surviving ships of the ARG, reinforced by some of the warships of TF 8, are currently undertaking a massive search and recovery mission where the ships or ARG 17 were killed or wounded.

"The Navy believes that the aliens no longer present a threat to their shipping from Mini Mouse. Perhaps they're right, at least in terms of the aliens having attack-capable warships there. But their ground attack on the squads we sent as security on the SAR missions to Mini Mouse suggests that they have an unknown but possibly substantial ground force still present on the small moon. The Navy is currently investigating, via satellite, both moons, looking for anomalies that could indicate alien installations.

"The Navy, incidentally, refers to them as 'the enemy,' almost as though they are in denial that they aren't human. We've all seen the vids, we know they aren't human.

"For all we know, the aliens are still right here on Troy, hidden in underground facilities. Many times in the past, the ancestors of our

Corps went up against enemies who lived and fought in caves. And died in them when Marines went in to dig them out. We have seen nothing to rule out the possibility that the aliens are underground.

"To that end, I want 3rd MAW to apply all possible resources to locating anomalies that could indicate caves or other sub-surface structures." That he directed at Major General Reginald Myers, the commander of 3rd Marine Air Wing. "G-2, use local geological studies and reports to locate possibly usable caves within one hundred klicks of Millerton." That was to Lieutenant Colonel Wendell Neville, his intelligence chief.

"In light of the fact that the remnants of ARG 17 and VII Corps are still in planetary space and not about to make planetfall, we will be on our own for the foreseeable future. So the rest of you, prepare your units to defend against attacks such as we saw in the vids of the initial invasion, and to attack when the aliens show themselves. At a time to be chosen by the enemy, we will be engaged with a foe of unknown strength and capabilities. I intend that the First Marine Combat Force will win.

"Brigadier General Porter, take over."

With that, Bauer marched out of the briefing room. Everybody rose to their feet and stood at attention until Porter called out,

"Seats!" and began giving his instructions.

Stasis Station A-1-53/S, NAUS Juno Beach

SECOND LIEUTENANT TED GREIG AWOKE; THE COMMANDER'S STASIS UNIT IN THE station Greig had led his platoon to automatically wake its occupant after two hours, unless ordered to do so at an earlier time.

As with the other two times he'd been in stasis, Greig needed a minute to clear his mind before he could move, or do anything other than groan. He pried his eyes open and sat up. A look around that wasn't as quick as he would have liked told him nobody else was awake yet. He levered himself out of the coffin-like stasis unit and stood on legs that quickly remembered how to stand and, eventually, walk.

Stasis can be a life-saver, he thought, *as long as you don't have to wake up fighting.*

He stretched, twisted left and right, and did a couple of deep knee bends to get himself moving again. Then he checked the time. Two hours since he'd locked his platoon down.

Two hours. The automatic commander's wake-up.

Where was the company commander, why hadn't he roused him, or the rest of the platoon? Or was that the responsibility of one of the ship's officers?

He tried his comm, but all he got was static. Things couldn't be *that* bad though—the ship's gravity was still on.

Greig looked to his left. Sergeant First Class Quinn's stasis unit was still closed; the platoon sergeant was still out. That needed to change, right now. Whatever Greig did, he was going to need help, and Quinn was the best help available.

In two steps, he was at the control panel for Quinn's unit. Waking him would be child's play: there were two pads on the panel, a green one with the word "UP" blazoned on it, and a red one labeled "DOWN." If "UP" didn't mean, "Rise up from stasis," whoever designed the panel didn't have a very good working knowledge of English. He tapped the green pad and was rewarded by the faint sounds of machinery from within the unit. After a moment the lid rose and he saw Quinn begin struggling to sit up.

"Take it easy, Sergeant," he said, putting a hand on Quinn's shoulder to keep him down. "Let it come naturally." He felt the sergeant's muscles relax.

Quinn worked his jaw, building saliva so he could speak. "Who's up?" he croaked.

"I don't know. Nobody answered my comm."

"Maybe your comm's broken?"

"Yeah, maybe." Greig didn't think so; the comm units were field hardened, supposed to stand up to the rigors of combat. His hadn't had any rough treatment at all.

"I don't think so either." Quinn took Greig's silence as disbelief of the comm being broken. His voice was stronger now, and he managed to sit up with little difficulty. "Gimme a hand." He reached, and Greig grasped his wrist and pulled him out of the unit. "You want me to wake the troops?"

Greig shook his head. "Not until we have a better idea of the situation. As soon as you're ready, let's go exploring."

"How much exploring can we do by ourselves? The ship has what, ten levels?"

"All we really have to explore is this deck, this is where our battalion is billeted. Only three decks are troops, the rest of the ship is ship operations and crew, or cargo."

"You're sure of that, LT?"

Greig nodded. "The *Juno Beach's* layout was covered in an officers call a couple of days before we left Earth. So like I said, we only need to look at this deck."

"Where are the vacuum suits?"

Greig looked a question at his platoon sergeant.

"We were under attack, LT, and nobody answered your comm. At the very least, the ship might have been holed and the atmosphere in the passage has gotten very thin."

When Greig didn't say anything, Quinn went on, "At worst, the ship's been destroyed and this station is drifting in vacuum.

Greig flinched. "Is that what you think happened? That the ship was destroyed, I mean?"

Quinn shrugged. "One thing I've learned in almost twenty years in this army is, when it comes to troop transports, anything's possible."

Greig gave a nervous chuckle. "I'm sure you're right. Let's find the vacuum suits."

The vacuum suits were right where they should be. The station had four rows of "coffins" with a locker at the ends of each row. The lockers held six vacuum suits apiece. The suits were intended for emergency use only, and were strictly intended for short time use. They came in four sizes that almost guaranteed that nobody could find one that fit properly. The one that Quinn got into was a marginally better fit than the one that sagged on Greig. The suits didn't look like the ones he'd seen sailors wearing when they went on EVA missions. They were far less form-fitting, and, instead of helmets, had hood arrangements with broad face plates that allowed the wearer's face to be clearly seen from outside.

"Are you ready, Sarge?" Greig asked over the suit's short-range comm once the two had attached the breathers to their backs.

"As ready as I'll ever be, LT." Quinn was less than two steps from the compartment's hatch. He ignored the display next to it and braced himself against the possible outrush of air if there was vacuum outside. He was staggered only slightly when he hit the "open" button and the airtight slid into a recess on the bulkhead: the atmosphere outside the compartment was thin enough that they needed the breathers, but far from vacuum.

Greig started to say, "I'll lead," but stopped when Quinn put out a hand to stop him and stepped into the doorway. Leaning so only his head and shoulders were outside, he looked both in both directions along the passageway.

"The emergency lights are on, but that's all I can see." He looked over his shoulder. "Which way, sir?"

Thinking quickly, remembering the basic plan of the ship, he said, "Go right." Right was forward, toward the front of the ship. The troop command compartments were forward of the troop compartments, the stasis compartments were aft, toward the rear. "There's another stasis compartment on the other side of this passage. Let's check it out first."

"Yes, sir."

Greig noticed that he had gone from being "LT" to "Sir." Evidently Quinn had decided to let the officer take full responsibility for what they were doing. That was fine by him. If he needed the platoon sergeant's advice at any point, he could ask for it.

The passageway was less than Spartan. It was painted battleship gray, top, bottom, and sides. Conduits and ducts ran the length of the overhead, tunneling through the bulkheads with airtight doors that divided the passageway into twenty-meter segments. Most of them were the same battleship gray as the walls. More anonymous gray conduits ran along the walls.

Stasis Station A-1-53/P was unoccupied; the lids on all the units were ajar. Just to be certain, Greig and Quinn quickly went through the compartment, looking inside each unit. Either nobody had reached the station, or they'd already gotten up and moved out. But if they had, why hadn't they woken him, or at least replied to his comm?

Back in the passageway, Greig tried his comm again.

"Static, nothing but static." Neither man commented on the lack of response, but it seemed possible that their platoon was the only survivors on board the *Juno Beach*.

The second hatch beyond the stasis compartment in which they'd ridden out the battle didn't open when Quinn hit the "open" button.

Greig swore under his breath—that probably meant there was vacuum on the other side of it. "Step back and grab hold of something," he said.

"Are you sure you want to do that, sir?"

"Got to be done. Now do what I said."

Greig watched Quinn take a few steps back and firmly grip a side duct and an overhead conduit. The sergeant fumbled shoving his gloved fingers behind the duct and conduit so he could get hold of them.

A small hatch was set into the bulkhead next to the airtight. A red lever was set in its middle, blazoned with the message, "Pulling this lever will sound alarms throughout this area of the starship and in all command and control compartments."

Greig braced himself into the corner where the passageway and hatch walls met, and pulled the red lever.

No alarm sounded, but the small hatch swung open, exposing manual controls for the airtight.

Greig took a steadying deep breath and flexed his fingers before slipping them onto the control dial. He twisted it.

And jerked back.

A voice boomed in the passageway: *"Warning! Warning! Opening this airtight is potentially dangerous! Make sure everything is secured before proceeding!"*

Greig looked back at Quinn. He could see his platoon sergeant had his eyes closed and his fingers twitched on the conduit and duct he held onto. He looked back at the manual controls and took another steadying deep breath.

"Here goes," he said softly, and turned the dial all the way to the "open" position. A *clunk* in the airtight told him it was unlocked and ready to be opened. He shoved a hand into the control box, reached the other to the "open" plate, and slapped it. The airtight made a grinding noise as it started sliding into its recess, but the noise quickly died out to silence, although Greig still felt the grinding through the metal. Evacuating air buffeted him as it rushed out of the short passageway into the void beyond.

The lieutenant waited until the air was no longer buffeting him, then, keeping a firm grip in the control box, leaned to the side to see though the now-open airtight.

Straight ahead was solid blackness, but to the left he saw stars. Some of the stars were moving; he thought they must be SAR craft looking for survivors. He hoped they weren't whoever had attacked the troop fleet. None seemed to be close to the *Juno Beach*. On the right, he faintly made out in starlight reflection the caved in bulkhead of the continuing passageway.

Miraculously, he was still being held to the deck by the ship's artificial gravity.

"Do you have a light, Sarge?" he asked, turning around to look at Quinn.

Quinn patted at his vacuum suit. "Can't find one," he said; his voice was weak. "What's there?"

"A big chunk of the ship's simply missing. But there might be a way forward. If I had a light I could find out."

Quinn's voice was suddenly more confident; the LT sounded like he knew what he was doing. "I think I saw lanterns in that empty compartment we checked out. I'll take a look, Sir."

"I'll be here." Then he had to hold tight again as the air in the next stretch of passageway evacuated past him.

When the buffeting of escaping atmosphere stopped, Greig tried his comm again. This time he thought he heard fragments of voices in the static. That encouraged him to try to raise somebody.

"Anyone who can hear, there are survivors on the *Juno Beach.* I'm Lieutenant Theodore W. Greig, Alpha Troop, First of the Seventh Mounted Infantry. My platoon is intact. I haven't been able to make contact with anybody else on board the ship, but my platoon sergeant and I are attempting to find other survivors. Any station, do you receive me? Over." He listened as intently as he could, but didn't hear anything that sounded like an attempt to reply to his transmission, not even when he repeated his message.

A bright beam of light suddenly flashed past Greig, illuminating the darkness beyond. He turned to see a grinning Quinn hustling toward him, a headlamp on his helmet and another in his hand. The one he wore was lit.

"I found two of these, sir!" Quinn stopped in front of the lieutenant and handed him the other lamp.

"Thanks, Sarge." Greig took the offered lamp and put it on before turning back to the void beyond the hatch, careful not to step through the opened door.

Whatever had been to the port side of the passageway was completely gone. The lantern showed jagged, bent edges of metal around the massive..."hole in the hull" seemed an inadequate description of the vacancy where just a couple of hours earlier compartments had existed, keeping the emptiness of space at bay. The gap extended to high above and halfway down, the strike must have come in from above the level of the passageway. It extended a full hundred meters beyond where Greig stood. A narrow ledge ran sporadically along the right side of what had been the passageway. Bits of the overhead were still there, similar to the remaining pieces of decking. Chunks of conduits and ductwork still hung onto the right side wall, but what had been on the ceiling was gone. The right side of the passageway wasn't intact; it was bowed away from the blast in places, and frequently holed. The wall on the far side of the gap was the same, deeply dented and holed.

Greig swallowed to moisten a suddenly dry throat, he doubted that anyone who might have been in the holed compartments had survived, not unless they were in stasis units. Even vacuum suits might not have saved them when the atmosphere blew out and slammed them through the holes, maybe shredding their suits on the jagged metal edges.

"What do you think, sir?"

"I think we can make it across there."

"Are you sure?" Quinn sounded doubtful.

"It looks like there's enough of the decking left, and we can hold onto the conduits to keep from falling away. So, yes, I think we can make it."

"Ah, LT? I'm surprised we've still got gravity here. You think there's gravity out there?"

Greig hesitated, then admitted, "I hadn't thought of that."

"We better find out before we go walking along."

"Right." Greig pulled himself fully into the doorway and extended a foot to the nearest piece of left over decking on the right wall.

He had to push his foot down to make contact, there was no gravity to pull him to it.

"It's pretty much free fall out here," he told Quinn. "Navy engineering is even more unbelievable than I imagined. How on earth do they manage to have artificial gravity in intact spaces, when it's missing in the next, holed space?"

"Got me on that one, sir." Quinn sounded like he thought Navy engineering was irrelevant to their situation.

Keeping hold of the frame over his head with his left hand, Greig reached for a conduit with his right and gave it a tug. It held.

"I'm going to try. Watch me. Follow if it seems safe."

"Shouldn't we have a rope of some sort, tie ourselves together?"

"That's a great idea, Sarge. But I haven't seen anything that looks like a rope. Have you?"

"Sorry. No I haven't. Be careful, sir."

Greig glanced out through the gap. Lights still moved around in the distance; what he thought were SAR teams rescuing survivors, just like before. And, the same as before, none were moving in the direction of the *Juno Beach*.

Making sure his right hand grip was firm, Greig reached with his left. He wanted to shuffle along, hands at shoulder level, feet on the remains of the deck, but the lack of gravity forced his legs to drift outward so he was angled away from the bulkhead rather than flush against it. He'd have to travel only using his hands. Unless he could find footholds along the way.

Ten meters along, he reached a punched hole that looked big enough for him to get though without catching himself on a jagged edge. It was.

Before entering, he looked at a sign on the wall. It read, "A-43-P." It was the troop compartment his platoon had been in. If he hadn't moved them to the stasis station, they'd all be dead now.

He decided not to mention that to Quinn. Bunks, lockers, cabinets, and other minor furnishings were jumbled about, funneling toward the opening. Everything was slowly settling to the deck. Personal belongings that had been left behind unsecured during the rapid abandonment of the compartment were mixed in with everything else. Greig felt a slight downward tugging, as of a very weak gravity field. *Amazing*, he thought.

"What do you have in there, sir?" Quinn asked, sounding worried.

He realized he had to tell his platoon sergeant. "This used to be our platoon's compartment." He hurried on before Quinn could react to the news. "I'm going to search, there might be something we can use. Maybe a stronger comm than the one I have." He didn't find a comm unit, but he did find a spool of electrical cable.

"Sarge, I've got something we can tie off with." He kept looking, now for something to use as a hook on the conduits, but came up dry.

A minute later, Quinn gingerly pulled himself through the opening in the bulkhead. They tied the cable around their waists with a ten meter length between them.

"Now if one of us goes, we both go," Quinn said.

"You're so encouraging, Sarge.

Quinn barked a short laugh.

Greig was surprised to find that he felt more secure tied to Quinn. If he lost his grip and drifted away the other could pull him back. Just as he could pull Quinn back if he lost his. But if they *both* somehow let go at the same time, or if something violently shook the ship and broke their grips, then they'd drift until someone picked them up. If someone picked them up. And if they were still alive.

Feeling more secure, he crawled faster along the wall, and it was only a few minutes before they reached the far side of the gap. The first hatch was broken, pushed in from its frame. It didn't take much effort to push it farther to admit them.

"The strike must have come from aft as well as above," Greig said. "That would explain why this wall and door are battered, but they're intact from the other side."

Quinn grunted. The direction the missile had come from was obvious enough it didn't need commenting on.

Twenty meters farther on they came to the end—the entire forward portion of the *Juno Beach* was missing, blown away by missiles that had zeroed in on the ship's bow.

"I've got a feeling we won't find anybody up ahead," Greig said to himself. He did his best not to show his dismay to Quinn, who was silent himself. He gathered himself and tried his comm again, beginning with identifying himself.

This time, he got an answer.

"Lieutenant Greig, this is Captain McMahan, Foxtrot, Second of the Tenth. Where are you?"

"Sir, I can't tell you how glad I am to hear your voice!"

"That's nice, Lieutenant, now where the fuck are you?"

"Yes, sir. We're on, on—. I don't know what deck this is, it's the one First Battalion was on. We're at what is now the forward edge of the *Juno Beach*..." His voice caught on that. "The wh-whole front end of the ship is missing."

"All right, I know where you're at. Now, you say 'we.' Who's we?"

"That's my platoon sergeant and me. The rest of the platoon is still in the stasis chamber. I left them in stasis while Sergeant Quinn and I try to find out what's happening."

"Have you located anybody else from your troop?"

"No, sir. We haven't seen anybody, and you're the first person to answer any of my comms."

"What stasis station is your platoon in?"

"We're in Alpha one dash fifty-three slash Sierra."

"You must have that wrong. Either that or you aren't as far forward as you said. Dash fifty-three is farther to the rear."

"Sir, we're as far forward as we can get—there's no ship in front of us."

"Wait one, I'm almost at the forward edge of what's left of the ship." A moment later Captain McMahan said, "I'm there. Go to the edge and look down. If you're all the way forward, you should see me two decks below you."

Greig took two steps to reach the end of the ship, grabbed something, and leaned out to look down.

"I see you, sir," he said and waved at the figure he saw leaning out two decks below.

"I see you too, Lieutenant," McMahan said. "Not far aft of here there's a big chunk blown out of the port side of the ship. The stasis station you said you came from is on the other side of it. Care to give me a different station number?"

"Sir, I know about the missing area. We were able to negotiate our way along a narrow strip of decking. Well, mostly we went hand over hand along conduits."

Greig could make out McMahan shake his head. "You're either very brave, or incredibly stupid," the captain said. "You think you can make it back to your station without killing yourselves?"

Greig looked at Quinn, who nodded.

"Yes, sir, we can do it."

"Then go there and wake your platoon. Right before I heard you, I made contact with SAR. They have us on their list and will be here in a couple of hours. So be ready to be rescued."

Greig and Quinn grinned at each other, relieved to know that someone knew where they were, and was coming for them.

Jordan, Eastern Shapland

DURING THE SAR MISSION TO MINI MOUSE, 3RD BATTALION, 1ST MARINES, moved to Jordan, one of the areas where Force Recon had encountered the aliens. India Company's Third platoon was held in reserve pending the return of its First squad. With the squad suffering two dead and three wounded out of its thirteen-man strength, Third platoon remained in reserve for the time being. Kilo Company was in positions on the north and west sides of Jordan, Lima Company on the south and east. Their lines were punctuated and backed up by the heavy weapons of Weapons Company. India Company was billeted inside the small city.

"Mackie, Cafferata," Sergeant Martin called out when he rejoined his squad after the squad leaders' debriefing that was held immediately after the return from Mini Mouse, "on me."

The two lance corporals heaved themselves to their feet from where they had been resting in the shade of a building on the south side of the town, and joined their squad leader. Neither was feeling very enthusiastic about anything, they didn't even feel relieved to be out of anything remotely resembling a defensive position.

"What's up, honcho?" Mackie asked flat-voiced when he reached Martin.

Cafferata didn't say anything, he just gave his squad leader a blank stare. The fight on Mini Mouse had been the first combat for either of them, the first time they'd lost men they knew. The experience was preying on them.

If Martin was depressed or upset by the casualties in his squad, it didn't show on his face or in his voice. "Both of your fire team leaders are out for a while with their wounds, but I guess you figured that."

Mackie mumbled an indistinct "I know," and Cafferata nodded dumbly.

"That means the two of you are acting fire team leaders, until Corporals Adriance and Button return to duty."

This time Mackie nodded dumbly, and Cafferata mumbled, "Yeah, I figured."

Martin looked closely at them, but neither looked back—or even at each other. Their eyes were down and to the side, not looking at anything in particular. He had to break them out of their funk before it got worse and paralyzed them.

"A-ten-*hut!*"

Startled by the unexpected command, the two came to attention, though not as sharply as they would have in garrison—or even before the fight on Mini Mouse.

"What i—?" Mackie started to say.

"Did I tell you to speak, Lance Corporal?" Martin snarled, thrusting his face into Mackie's. He shot a glare at Cafferata, warning him to keep quiet. "Well?" he demanded when Mackie didn't say anything.

"No, Sergeant," Mackie said, clench jawed. His eyes were fixed straight ahead.

Martin took a step back and looked from one to the other before saying, "Listen up, you two, and listen up good. Do you think you're the 1st Marines to lose buddies in combat? *Every* Marine who's gone in harm's way has lost buddies. I have, Sergeant Johnson has, and Sergeant Mausert has. And you better believe Staff Sergeant Guillen has! Some of the corporals in this platoon have lost buddies in combat. I know it's shitty, but shit happens, particularly in war."

He stopped and looked aside for a moment. When he began again, his voice was thick. "I just lost two more Marines, men I was responsible for." His voice harshened. "If you feel like hell, how do you think I feel? Zion and Porter were my men, my responsibility. That weighs, that weighs heavily. Heavier than what's got you down, believe me.

"But if I let it weigh me down too much, it'll make me screw up somehow the next time we meet those aliens, and more Marines will get killed. Then it won't just be because shit happens, it'll be because I screwed up. Their deaths will my fault. I can't allow that to happen. And I can't allow you to feel so sorry for yourselves that you screw up and get good Marines killed. So shape up! Do you understand? *Do you?*"

Mackie swallowed rather than say anything. Cafferata mumbled, "Yes, Sergeant."

Martin again shoved his face to Mackie's. "Do you hate me, Mackie? Is that why you aren't getting with the program?"

Mackie worked up a mouthful of nervous saliva, then swallowed it. "No, Sergeant, I don't hate you. I'm thinking about the squad, how we can function when we're short so many men." His voice was clear, although not as strong as he would have liked.

"Oh?" Martin said, taking a step back. "Do you have a suggestion, Lance Corporal?"

"Ah..." Mackie looked around, thinking.

"I'm waiting, Lance Corporal."

"Well, we're down five men. That leaves us—you—with seven men. Wouldn't reorganizing the squad into two fire teams be better?"

"You mean with me as one fire team leader and Corporal Vittori as the other?"

"Yes, Sergeant, sort of like that."

Martin slowly shook his head. "No, for a couple of reasons. First, our wounded will be coming back fairly soon, and I don't want to have to keep reorganizing the squad. Second, I want to give my lance corporals a bit of experience as fire team leaders—."

"But First fire team is only me and Orndoff! Third fire team is Cafferata and Hill. And what about experience for Garcia, he's a lance corporal, too."

Martin nodded. "That's true, all of what you said. But you and Cafferata only having one man each limits how much you can screw up. And getting Garcia some experience is my problem, not yours, so don't worry about it. Do you remember that exercise in Hawaii, when you wound up being an acting fire team leader when I was a simulated casualty?"

"Yes, Sergeant." Mackie swallowed again.

"That was training. This is real. It's different. Do you understand?"

Mackie's eyes widened. "Yes, Sergeant."

"That's better. Now, are you ready to take on a little responsibility?"

"Yes, Sergeant!"

"What about you, Cafferata?"

"Yes, Sergeant, I am." Cafferata beamed.

Satisfied that the two had no further questions, Martin called out, "First squad, on me!" In a moment the other five members of the squad were standing in front of him. He briefly updated them on the condition of their three wounded Marines and told them how he was reorganizing the squad.

"It's only temporary," he finished. "Corporal Vittori is the senior man, both in rank and experience, so make no mistake, he's second to me in the squad's chain of command regardless of who's First fire team leader. Any questions?"

The question was almost always rhetorical, and was so this time as well—nobody had any questions.

"All right, then. The situation remains the same; India Company is in reserve for the battalion, Second platoon is reserve for the company, and First squad is the platoon's reserve. We'll be the last ones committed if, and I emphasize *if* the aliens attack here."

"I have a question now, Sergeant Martin," Mackie said.

"You couldn't have asked it before?"

Mackie shook his head. "Before was about the squad's reorganization. This is about our reserve status."

"So what's your question?"

"How good is the intelligence that the aliens aren't likely to attack here?"

Martin gave Mackie a hard look, then glanced around to see if any officers or senior NCOs were near by. None were. He motioned everybody to close in.

"All right," he said *sotto voce*, "here's the straight scoop, so far as I know it. Nobody, not recon, Force Recon, air, or satellite, has found the aliens or signs that they were just here.

"But.... Here's where it gets hairy. I've heard scuttlebutt that satellite observation has discovered gravitational anomalies similar to the ones on Mini Mouse, the ones where the aliens came from to attack us when we went in with the SAR birds." He shrugged. "I know, and you probably do too, that all worlds have gravitational anomalies, and they don't necessarily mean squat. But we also know that on Mini Mouse some of the anomalies indicated hiding places for the aliens. What that means is, maybe nobody's here to bother us. Maybe the aliens have us outnumbered and are just waiting for us to let our guards down."

He stepped back and allowed his voice to move back toward normal. "That's everything I know or have heard. What I suspect is, we had best be alert, because those little bad bastards could come at us from anywhere at any time. It doesn't matter that we're in reserve. When they hit, they're just as likely to hit us here as hit anybody at Millerton. And they could even pop up right here inside Jordan, so that India Company would be the First Marines engaged.

"Any more questions? No? Good! So don't give me any shit the next time I tell you to clean your weapons. Now get back to whatever goofing off you were doing. Just keep an eye peeled for trouble, that's all.

"And clean your damn weapons!"

Before the end of the day, the Marines of India Company were moved into the vacant houses in Jordan.

Settling in, Jordan

Over the next three days reports filtered down to the Marines planetside about elements of VII Corps being located and rescued by Navy Search and Rescue teams. The Army troops were being apportioned to the serviceable transports of ARG17 to continue their voyage to Troy. There were no reports of sightings of the enemy, in space, on Mini Mouse, or planetside.

Three days. That's how long it took for Sergeant Martin to become a prophet.

Number 8, Sugar Clover Place, Jordan, Eastern Shapland

"What the fuck!" Orndoff shouted. He scrabbled across the floor of the house's living room, reaching for his rifle.

"What's the problem?" Mackie asked. He already had his rifle in his hands by the time he looked past Orndoff and saw an alien crouched in the doorway to the dining room, pointing its weapon ahead of itself. The alien looked just like the images they'd studied on their way to Troy—head at the end of a long neck, body horizontal on top of legs that bent the wrong way, feather-like structures ran from its crown down the length of its back until they blossomed into a spray on its tail.

"Oh, shit!" Mackie shouted. He didn't hesitate but began shooting even before he had his rifle trained on the intruder. The alien got off a short, automatic burst from its weapon before bullets from Mackie's rifle blew it out of the doorway.

"First squad, report!" Sergeant Martin shouted from somewhere else in the house. Pounding footsteps said that he was running toward the fire.

"First fire team, we're all right," Mackie shouted after glancing at Orndoff to make sure he hadn't been injured in the brief exchange of fire.

While Vittori and Cafferata were reporting no casualties in their fire teams, Mackie positioned Orndoff.

"Get behind the divan and cover me."

"Where are you going?" Orndoff shouted.

Martin burst into the room and swept it with his eyes. "What happened, Mackie? And where are you going?" Martin demanded.

Mackie paused on his way to the door where the alien had appeared and looked at his squad leader, noticing that Martin hadn't taken the time to grab his helmet. "An alien just came in. I blew him away. Now I'm going to see where he went."

Martin had heard Mackie tell Orndoff what to do. He spared the PFC a glance to judge his angle of covering fire, then said, "I'm coming with you, from the other side. Where's your helmet?"

"The same place as yours."

"Let's do it."

The two approached the doorway at different angles, neither straight ahead. Mackie from the left, looking through the door to the right, Martin from the right looking into the area to the left of the doorway.

"Do you see it?" Martin asked.

"It's not in my field of view."

"Did it come out of the kitchen?" Martin asked. The kitchen was the only other room that entered into the dining room. Martin had reached the door and was against the wall to the right, looking as deep into the room as possible. A china cabinet and a credenza were against the walls, too close for anyone to hide behind. The dining table had a cloth, but it barely overlapped the table top, providing no way to hide underneath. Neither did the chairs placed around the table obstruct the view.

"I don't know. It was already in the doorway by the time I saw it." He was opposite Martin at the doorway. Between them they could see nearly the entire interior of the dining room.

"You ready?" Martin asked. When Mackie nodded, he said, "On three, you then me. One. Two. *Three!*"

Mackie charged through the doorway left to right, spinning to cover the corner he hadn't been able to see into. Martin was right behind him, going right to left and covering the corner he hadn't seen into.

"Clear," Mackie shouted.

"Clear," Martin echoed.

The alien wasn't there. But...

"I have a blood trail," Mackie said.

"And I've got a weapon," Martin said. Turning his head back to the living room, he called, "Orndoff, get in here. Secure that." He pointed to the alien's—rifle, for lack of a better name to call it. Then he got on his comm to report to Second Lieutenant Commiskey.

After reporting the bare bones of what had already happened, he said, "We've secured the weapon and are following the blood trail into the kitchen. There's an exit to the backyard there, maybe it came from outside."

"When you find where it went next," Commiskey said, "don't pursue. Report, then we'll decide what to do next."

"Aye aye, report but don't pursue."

Commiskey signed off, presumably to report to Captain Sitter.

"Orndoff," Martin said, "cover us. Mackie, let's check the kitchen the same way we came in here."

"Roger that, honcho." Mackie answered. He froze a soon as he turned to check the corner.

"The basement door's open," he said softly. "And I found the body."

"Orndoff, get in here and give us some cover," Martin said.

Orndoff came in carrying the alien's rifle in his left hand and his own in his right.

"Put the alien weapon down and hold your rifle like you know how to use it, Orndoff," Mackie snapped.

Martin got on his comm. "Vittori, get your fire team into the dining room, it looks like the alien came through the kitchen from the basement. Cafferata, I want you and your fire team in the living room." He waited for them to "roger," then reported to Commiskey.

When he was through on his comm, he joined Mackie to examine the alien corpse. It was sprawled, both arms reaching toward the open basement door. One leg stretched out behind, the other cocked as though it had been pushing itself forward one leg at a time. Blood, a red similar to human blood but somehow not the same red, was pooled around it, but no more seemed to be leaking out of any of its wounds.

"You got your tie downs on you?" Martin asked.

"Always," Mackie said, handing Martin one of the ties that the Marines used to bind prisoners, or secure anything else that needed to be secured.

Martin looped one end in a hasty knot around the alien's trailing foot, then backed out of the kitchen. Mackie went ahead of him. In the dining room, with a wall between them and the alien, Martin gave the cord a sharp jerk, then a more steady pull, until he was confident the corpse had moved at least a meter.

"I guess he didn't booby-trap himself," Mackie said.

"Always check to make sure," Martin said. He stood to return to the kitchen, and reeled back, shouting, "Aliens!"

There was no place to go for cover, he dropped to a knee and started firing through the kitchen door.

"Everybody, into the living room!" Martin shouted. "Take cover there." He kept firing rapidly into the kitchen. It was enough to keep the aliens he'd seen rushing out of the basement from coming farther.

A chittering voice, commanding even though it was in a higher register than a human's, shouted from out of sight, probably at the head of the basement stairs. Several high-pitched voices answered it, they sounded like protests, enlisted who didn't want to go into a fire storm.

"Somebody, throw a grenade in there!"

"I got it!" Mackie shouted. He armed a grenade, and bowled it along the floor so that it ricocheted off the jam and spun behind the wall toward the basement door.

The voices in the kitchen erupted in high-pitched jabbering, accompanied by the scrabbling of something hard—claws?—on the floor. The grenade exploded, setting off shrill cries, and more commanding shouts.

Martin took advantage of the aliens' momentary confusion to dash out of the dining room, into the living room. He got on his comm to report, and only then heard the reports from the rest of the platoon; all three of the houses the platoon was divided into were under attack from aliens that came up from the basements.

"Cafferata," Martin shouted, "look out the windows, watch for aliens. Mackie, take Orndoff and check the bedrooms, then get back in here."

Shouts and scrabbling from beyond the dining room announced that the aliens in the kitchen were about to charge into sight.

"Get ready!" Vittori shouted to his men.

"Orndoff, let's go!" Mackie shouted as he raced for the bedroom hallway. There were three bedrooms along a hallway behind the living room. The first one's door was halfway open. Mackie slammed into the door to smash anyone hiding behind it into the wall and spun away into the middle of the room, looking all around for aliens. Orndoff was close behind him.

"Orndoff, check the closet, I'll cover you."

"Right." Orndoff darted to the closet and slammed its sliding door to the side. He jabbed into its corners with his rifle muzzle, but met only clothing. As soon as he announced the closet was clear, Mackie dropped down and looked under the bed. It was clear except for dust bunnies. After looking out the windows and not seeing anyone, human or alien, they ran into the next bedroom, anxious to finish their search and get back to the living room, where they heard an increasing volume of gunfire.

"The bedrooms are clear," Mackie reported to Martin when he and Orndoff returned. "We looked outside. Didn't see anybody, but it sounds like every occupied house has a fire fight going on inside." He wanted to ask how things were going here, but the four alien bodies in the doorway to the dining room and continued high pitched shouts from just out of sight told him all he needed to know.

"Do you think you can bounce another grenade in there?" Martin asked him.

"I can give it a try."

"Just don't bounce it to someplace it'll hit us."

"No sweat." Mackie moved to his right as he readied a grenade. He judged his angle, then cocked his arm and threw the grenade hard enough to spin wildly out of sight behind the wall where the alien voices came from. Before it went off, three aliens shot through the doorway, faster than the Marines could point their weapons at the rapidly moving forms and fire. In the dining room, voices rose to a new pitch just before the grenade went off. After it exploded, there were far fewer voices.

But three aliens were in the living room with the Marines. One of them leaped on Lance Corporal Fernando Garcia and another attacked Cafferata, trying to get beyond him to the window. The third darted around aimlessly.

Garcia luckily managed to get his rifle up to block the leaping alien that swung talons on the ends of its short arms at him. The Marine's arms were enough longer to keep the talons from ripping into his chest, but they gouged deep furrows in both of his arms, sending blood shooting out. PFC Harry Harvey, a bare meter away, slammed the butt of his rifle into the alien's head, knocking it away from Garcia before it could do any further damage to the wounded Marine. Orndoff was close enough that he could reach Garcia before anybody else. He ran to the wounded Marine and yanked the draperies from the windows to wrap around Garcia's arms to staunch the bleeding.

Dazed, the alien was slow getting back to its feet, but that short delay was all Harvey needed to drop his rifle and get to it to snap its neck over his knee, the way Mackie had killed one of the aliens on Mini Mouse. The alien went into spasms, and its arms and legs flailed about, its head flopping about from the break in its neck. Harvey picked up his rifle, stomped on the alien's neck just below its jaw, and shot it in the head. Its spasms stopped. Harvey turned to Garcia, and found that Orndoff was already stopping the bleeding.

Cafferata was turning to see what was going on inside the room when the alien jumped at him, so it didn't hit him with its full force. It was still enough to knock him away from the window. The alien ignored the Marine now that he wasn't blocking the window; it tried to jump through it, but bounced back—it hadn't realized the clear glass meant the window was closed—right into Hill, who grabbed it high on its neck and whirled around. Something snapped, and the alien let out a distressed *caw*. It ran about chaotically, its head swinging from its high-held neck, until Cafferata swung his rifle at its legs, taking them out from under it. Hill jumped feet first on the alien's chest. Bones snapped loudly.

The third alien suddenly stopped its aimless dashing about and looked at the situation it found itself in. Six Marines were facing it, holding their weapons ready to use one way or another to bring it down.

Martin was the only one who hadn't been involved with the other aliens, and was waiting for the alien to stop long enough for him to get off a shot. He fired just as the alien bolted for the bedroom hallway. He missed.

Mackie heard the shot and turned to look. The alien was jinking side to side as it sped down the hallway, but the hall was narrow enough that it couldn't dodge widely. Mackie began firing after it, as did Martin. They were never later able to tell which of them hit the alien, but it crashed to the floor, bleeding profusely. Mackie ran to it, knocked its weapon out of reach, and put a bullet through its head.

"Cease fire!" Martin ordered. When everybody stopped shooting, he listened very carefully. Gunfire and the shouts of Marines in battle came from other houses, but he didn't hear any noises in his squad's house other than the small noises his squad was making.

"Mackie, give 'em another grenade."

"Aye aye, honcho." Mackie stepped to the side of the dining room door and threw a grenade hard around the jam. No cries, no scrabbling joined the *thunking* of the grenade as it bounced in the room, no cries followed the explosion.

Martin got on his comm to report to Commiskey. It took a moment for the lieutenant to answer his call.

"Report, One," Commiskey said over the background sound of gunfire.

"We seem to have beaten them off, Six. What the hell's going on over there?" Martin replied.

"Same as with you, One. Everybody got hit. We're driving them back."

Martin shuddered. "Do you have any casualties?"

"Only one. Doc's patching him now. How many do you have?"

"Also one WIA." Martin looked at Garcia; the bandages on his wounds seemed to be holding. "I think he'll be all right until a corpsman can get to us."

"It shouldn't be a long wait." It sounded that way to Martin, the fire was slackening off.

"I'll let you know when Doc's on his way. Have you checked the entire house yet?"

"No, sir, that's my next step."

"Do it, then report back. Six out."

Martin looked at Mackie, nodded toward the dining room and said, "Take a look."

Mackie took a deep, steadying breath, and flung himself through the doorway, to land prone on the floor next to the dining table, facing the kitchen and aiming his rifle at the door.

"Second fire team, collect the weapons," Martin ordered.

Vittori and his two men gathered the aliens' weapons, first the ones in the doorway, then the ones near the dozen dead or dying in the dining room. They piled the weapons in the living room, away from the dining room door, and stacked the bodies at the end of the dining room opposite the kitchen. Two of the aliens were still alive. Martin ordered their hands tied off, and for them to be placed back to back, with their elbows lashed together.

"Think they'll survive?" Vittori asked.

"I don't give a good goddam," Martin said. He glanced at the two, bleeding from multiple wounds. "How's Garcia?" he asked Orndoff.

"He's been better."

"I'll be fine as soon as a corpsman dresses my wounds," Garcia said.

"Sure you will," Martin said, but he didn't believe it. Garcia's voice was weak, and he looked pale from blood loss. "Doc's on his way."

Turning to the rest of the squad, Martin said, "All right, let's check out the kitchen and the basement. If these two are still alive after that, we'll see what we can do about stopping their bleeding."

There were another five bodies in the kitchen and three more on the stairs to the basement.

The basement was one large, bare room.

"All right, where'd they come from?" Martin said. There weren't any exits other than the stairs the Marines had come down. "Nobody was here when we moved in. So how the hell'd they get down here?"

Nobody had an answer.

"We need the engineers to check this place out."

They had killed nearly twenty of the aliens and captured two more. Garcia was the only wounded Marine. They had trouble believing their good luck.

"We had experience from Mini Mouse," Martin told his men. "If it hadn't been for that, we most likely would have lost more men just now." He looked at the stacked corpses. "Maybe none of them had combat experience."

Expeditionary Air Field, Jordan, Eastern Shapland

LIEUTENANT COLONEL RAY DAVIS, COMMANDING OFFICER OF 3RD BATTALION, 1st Marines, watched from inside the operation center as four speeding dots resolved into four Marine Kestrels that took station orbiting the expeditionary air field a couple of hundred meters above the ground, ready to pounce on any threat. Another division of four Kestrels began orbiting higher up, watching for any threat that might approach on land or in the air. A C126VEC "Bulldog," VIP transport/electronic warfare/command and control aircraft following the Kestrels touched down and came to a stop a hundred meters away from the OpCen. Only then did Davis step outside. He did his best to ignore the buffeting wind, even though the wind was what had kept him inside until nearly the last minute. The hatch on the side of the Bulldog opened just as a short stairway rolled up to it. A Marine appeared in the open hatch, looked around, fixed on Davis, and marched down the stairs. Another Marine, and a third followed him and marched just to his rear and left when they reached the field's decking.

Davis met them halfway, came to attention and raised his right hand in salute. "Welcome to Marine Corps Station Jordan, sir," he said. The wind almost blew his words away.

Lieutenant General Bauer crisply returned the salute, paused for 1st Marines' commander Colonel Justice Chambers to trade salutes with Davis, then gripped his hand with both of his to shake. Chambers returned the salute of Bauer's aide, Captain Upshur.

"You beat them all off successfully?" Bauer asked without preamble as the three started toward a waiting ground car—they had to lean into the wind.

"My men did, sir." Davis shook his head. "Most of the action was inside the houses where individual squads were billeted. There was very little I or any other officers could do to affect the fighting—especially as most command elements were also under attack and fighting off the aliens."

Bauer shook his head. Not in disbelief, but in something closer to awe. "It was a squad leader's war."

"It certainly was, sir. Even when they hit in Officer Country, the command elements had to fight like squads."

"Most of the command elements were attacked?"

"Nearly every one of them, sir."

"And every attack came from inside the houses?

"From the basements, yes, sir."

The driver of the ground car stood holding the door firmly with one hand to keep the wind from banging it against the vehicle's side. He didn't stand at attention or salute, and his rifle was in his other hand while he looked around for threats. The three officers entered the car, Davis then Chambers with Bauer last.

When they were seated, Bauer asked, "Is it usually that windy here?"

"No, sir. It's just that the ground has been so thoroughly cleared around the air field that there's nothing to break the wind."

Bauer nodded his understanding, then got to the reason he was visiting the Marines in Jordan.

"You haven't found any way they could have gotten into the basements before the attacks?"

"That's right, sir. That's why I requested engineers with ground penetrating radar. There have to be tunnels below the houses, and hidden entrance into the basements. So far, none of my people have been able to find an egress."

"You're going to show me some of the houses." It wasn't a question.

"Our first stop is one of the houses India Company's Third platoon was in. It was one of the most successful at fighting off the aliens."

Bauer thought for a moment. "India's First platoon. One of its squads wiped out a couple of squads worth of the aliens on Mini Mouse, didn't it?"

"Yes, sir. The very squad we're about to visit, as a matter of fact."

"And they were one of the most successful in repelling the aliens here?"

"That's right, sir."

Bauer grunted. "Experience makes all the difference in the world."

Number 8, Sugar Clover Place, Jordan, Eastern Shapland

"Attention on deck!" Lance Corporal Mackie shouted when he saw Bauer and the other officers step onto the house's veranda. He raced to the door, threw it open, and stepped aside at attention. Bauer graced him with a curt nod as he walked in.

"Who's in command here?" he asked.

"Second Lieutenant Commiskey, sir," Davis answered.

"Were you in this house during the fight, Mr. Commiskey?" Bauer asked.

"No, sir. That was Sergeant Martin," Commiskey said. "He was in command here during the fight."

"You were involved in your own firefight at the time?"

"That's right, sir."

"We'll get to that later. Right now I want to find out about this one." Bauer looked at the other Marines in the room. "Sergeant Martin?"

"Here, sir." Martin took a step toward the general.

"Walk me through it, Sergeant."

"Aye aye, sir. It started when Lance Corporal Mackie, he's the one by the door, saw a Duster in the doorway..."

"Duster?" Bauer interrupted Martin.

"Yes, sir. Those feather things on their tails make them look like feather dusters. So we're calling them 'Dusters' for short."

"This squad has had more contact with them than any other, you've earned the right to name them. So that's what I'll call the aliens, too. Dusters. Continue, please."

"Yes, sir. Mackie saw a Duster in the dining room door and blew him away."

"Sir," Mackie said, "by your leave, General, sir, it was PFC Orndoff who saw the Duster first."

"But you shot it?"

"Yes, sir, I did."

"Very good." Bauer turned back to Martin. "You were saying, Sergeant."

"Right, sir. After PFC Orndoff saw the Duster and Lance Corporal Mackie shot it... ." Martin related the battle, showing Bauer the captured weapons, the blood stains on the flooring, and the rooms the action took place in, finishing in the basement. "We can't figure out how they got down here. There has to be a hidden doorway, because we checked this place from top to bottom when we first moved in, and the basement was empty."

"Are you saying you checked because you wanted to make sure there wasn't anybody hiding here?"

"No, sir," Martin said with an embarrassed laugh. "We were looking to see if there was anything left behind that we could use."

"Of course. Now, where are the bodies?"

"They're in the back, sir," Commiskey said, "waiting to be picked up."

"Show me."

Behind the house were two rows of bent corpses; legs that wouldn't go straight along the axis of the bodies, long necks that held serpentine curves even in death. There were ten corpses in each row, naked except for leather-like straps with pouches on them.

Bauer looked at Martin. "Now your casualties."

"Lance Corporal Garcia, sir." Martin indicated a Marine with bandaged arms. "He's the only one."

"And you had two prisoners?"

"*Had* is the right word, sir. One of them died. That one." He pointed to a corpse at the end of the nearer row. "Battalion S2 collected the live one."

Bauer spent a moment looking at the alien corpses, then at Garcia.

"Mr. Commiskey, how many casualties did your platoon have in total?"

"Sir, we had two KIA and six wounded, including Lance Corporal Garcia."

"Against how many aliens?"

"More than sixty, sir."

Bauer nodded, as though to himself. "All in confined spaces, rather than in the open."

"That's right, sir."

The general turned back to Martin. "You have an outstanding squad, Sergeant. He looked at the rest of the squad. "All of you. You performed here today in the highest tradition of the Marine Corps." Back to Martin: "Is there anything you could have used to make your victory more decisive?"

"Yes, sir, there is." Martin glanced at the bodies. "They move fast, and really jink when they run. Just like in the vids we saw onboard ship coming here, and like we ran into on Mini Mouse. We need scatter guns. Weapons that will hit a rapidly moving target with something other than a lucky shot. If they hadn't been in confined spaces, if they'd been able to move like they can in the open, we might have been in serious trouble."

"I'll see what I can do. Semper Fi, Marines. Let me say again, you did an outstanding job." Bauer turned to walk around the side of the house.

"I want to see a couple more squads, make sure one of them is one that didn't do so well," Bauer said to Davis. "I also want to see a company command element and your headquarters."

He said to Upshur, "Make a note, I am requesting thirty thousand shotguns, and a month's supply of ammunition for them."

Back to Davis, "I understand that your command elements had higher casualty rates than the squads did, is that correct?"

"Yes, sir, it is," Davis said, sounding distinctly unhappy. "I lost twenty-three officers and seventeen staff NCOs. Most of the elements were smaller than the squads, and none of them were as well armed."

"Do whatever reorganizing you have to in order to rebuild your command structures. I'll see what I can do about replacing officers and senior NCOs." He paused in thought for a second. "Some of the losses can be made up with promotions and brevet commissions from the ranks. Look into who deserves it."

They reached the ground car. Bauer paused before getting in, looking at the sky and surrounding trees. "It's amazing how trees can cut down on the wind."

After Davis gave the driver direction to their next stop, Bauer asked Davis about the rest of the battalion's casualties.

"In addition to the casualties in the various command groups, I lost more than fifty NCOs and junior enlisted, both KIA and wounded badly enough to require evacuation to ship-board medical facilities."

Bauer refrained from asking how many aliens had died. "Let's get on with this show."

Admiral's Cabin, NAUS Durango, in Orbit Around Troy

Ships of the NAU Navy that were configured for flagship designation had marvelous capabilities undreamt of by any other than the most pie-in-the-sky dreamers of earlier naval planners. Among them was the automatic monitoring of all friendly communications in nearby space, including planetary surfaces and atmospheres. And monitor surface communications was exactly what Rear Admiral Avery did during the alien attack on the Marines in Jordan.

"Distraught" was not too strong a word to use in describing Avery's state of mind at the time. He was still extremely upset over the nearly total loss of ARG 17 and still blamed himself for the loss. As distraught as Admiral Avery was, and as intent as he was on listening to the communications among the squads in Jordan, it didn't occur to him to also monitor communications from the Marines in and around Millerton and the McKinzie Elevator Base. If it had occurred to him, and if he had acted on it, he would have realized that the only combat was in Jordan, and only involved one battalion of Marines—a fairly small portion of the Marine strength on Troy.

Being distraught and possessing only limited intelligence is a very bad combination for a commander—it can lead to mistakes.

Avery made a mistake. More than one, as a matter of fact.

His first was continuing to blame himself for the loss of most of ARG17. After paying attention to an entirely too small part of Troy, he blamed himself for the alien attack on the Marines in Jordan, and—without consulting anyone more familiar with ground combat than he was—assumed the results of the battle were worse than they in fact were.

His greatest mistake was concluding that the Marines planetside were being defeated, were about to be driven out of their planethead. Or at least from Jordan and probably all of Eastern Shapland.

He quickly, again without conferring with anyone, prepared a message to be sent via drone to the North American Union's Supreme Military Headquarters on Earth. After drawing a bleak picture of what had happened to ARG17 and was happening planetside the message concluded:

Issue in doubt.

Three words immediately recognizable to anyone familiar with the first days of the old United States of America's involvement in the world-spanning war that took place in the middle of the twentieth century.

First MCF Headquarters, Outside Millerton

"Captain Upshur," Bauer said as he entered his HQ building, "prepare a message to send to Earth via Navy drone. I don't care if they have to open a wormhole for just this purpose."

Upshur positioned his comp to take the information needed for Bauer's message. "Ready, sir."

"You heard the replacements Chambers and Davis asked for? Double the number. You have my note about shotguns and shells? Add a month's supply of grapeshot for our artillery. Add a company of engineers with lots of ground penetrating radar and tunneling equipment. Say why I want them. Got it all?"

"All of it, sir."

"Hand deliver it to Townsend on the *Durango*. I don't want to take the chance of it getting misplaced, or put into routine routing."

"Aye aye, sir. By your leave?"

"Go. Let me know when you get back."

Comm Shack, NAUS Durango, in Orbit

"Captain Upshur!" Lieutenant Townsend exclaimed on seeing Bauer's aide. "What brings you to orbit?"

"Lieutenant," Upshur said, extending a hand to his Navy counterpart. "I heard a rumor, probably false, that the Navy has excellent coffee, and thought I'd come up for a mug of it."

Townsend laughed. "Not false. The NAU Navy has the best coffee in the entire universe. And you're more than welcome to a mug—or more. Let's head for the ward room and you can tell me why else you're here."

"Before we go to the ward room for some of that delicious coffee, I need a favor. Or General Bauer needs it."

"Oh? And what might the distinguished general want?"

Upshur drew a crystal from his jacket pocket. "A message to SecWar and the President."

"Has Admiral Avery seen it?" Townsend said, taken aback.

Upshur shook his head. "Not unless he radioed a copy to him since I left his HQ. He said he doesn't want this to get bogged down in any routine handling. He also said that if necessary I should make you open a wormhole to send it."

Townsend considered the crystal before taking it. "All right. It so happens that a wormhole is opening in a few hours. I just sent a drone to Earth from the admiral. I can send off another drone right now and it should reach the wormhole before it closes again."

"Thanks, Julius. You've just earned the gratitude of a Marine lieutenant general."

"Not something to be taken lightly." Townsend set about getting the crystal into a drone for immediate launch for Earth.

The ward room coffee was just as good as rumored.

The War Room, Supreme Military Headquarters,
Bellevue, Sarpy County, Federal Zone, NAU

A day after Admiral Avery's two messages about the attack on ARG17 reached Earth, his "issue in doubt" message arrived.

It took a week for the messages to reach Earth, where they were promptly delivered to NAU President Mills and Secretary of War Hobson. Hobson took no action on receipt of the initial messages; he needed more information. But when he read the third one...

Knowing that the President didn't necessarily read his messages from offworld as soon as he received them, Hobson chose to call him rather than wait for the President to contact him first. He was right, Mills hadn't yet gotten around to reading the message.

"'Issue in doubt,' what does that mean?" Mills asked when he finished reading.

"It means, sir, that Admiral Avery thinks the Marines on Troy will be defeated by the aliens."

There was silence for a moment before Mills asked somewhat shakily, "When was the last time that happened? That anybody defeated our Marines?"

Hobson didn't have to think about it, he knew. "Not in my lifetime or yours."

"Then how can it happen this time?"

"We went in having no idea of the enemy's strength. If there are enough of them, or if they're heavily enough armed, they could do it."

"So what can we do?

"I don't know yet. Nobody but you and I know about Avery's messages. I am meeting with the Joint Chiefs this afternoon."

"Now, now this message is from the Navy commander. What does the Marine commander have to say about the situation?"

"We haven't heard from General Bauer. For all I know, he was killed in the action Avery describes."

"Gods," Mills murmured, remembering the pics and vids he'd seen of the original alien attack on Troy. He pulled himself together and asked in a firm voice, "Didn't you order a large follow-on force to be stood up?"

"Yes, I did. The Second Army."

"What's its status?"

"Its command structure is in place, and most of its component elements have been identified. The Navy is still working on finding enough shipping to transport that large a force."

"How long will it be before Second Army will be ready to go?"

Hobson stifled a sigh. As knowledgeable as Mills was in political matters, he was quite ignorant about the military.

"That's not the question," he said with more patience than he felt. "The right question is, what are we up against on Troy. Until we hear from General Bauer, or whoever is the ranking remaining Marine on the ground, we simply don't know enough to even make a guess."

Mills took a deep breath. "All right, what are you going to do?"

"As I said, I'm meeting with the Joint Chiefs this afternoon. Then we will begin deciding what to do."

Mills took another deep breath. "Keep me appraised," he said.

"I will do that, Mr. President. I most assuredly will." *And if things go to hell in a handbasket, I'll assuredly find a way to lay the blame on you.*

The War Room, Supreme Military Headquarters,
Bellevue, Sarpy County, Federal Zone, NAU

IGNATZ GRESSER WAS ALREADY WAITING IN THE WAR ROOM WHEN THE JOINT
Chiefs of Staff's Director of Intelligence, Major General Joseph de
Castro, arrived.

"Mr. Gresser," de Castro greeted the President's special assistant.

"General," Gresser said with a nod. He rose from the seat he was
occupying at the foot of the long table and extended his hand to de
Castro. It was the kind of handshake exchanged between men who
know each other mostly by reputation rather than men who know and
respect each other personally.

"You're the intelligence guy, right?" Gresser asked once they were
both seated. De Castro, the lowest ranking military man who
would attend the meeting was also at the lower end of the table.

"They've been calling me that for most of my career," de Castro
said with a chuckle, "but you're the first civilian to use that term on
me."

"I hope I didn't offend you."

"Not at, not at all. Intelligence is my game. To demonstrate, I
sensed another question behind that one."

Gresser nodded. "Intelligence on more than one sense, eh? You're
right, President Mills got the distinct impression from SecWar that
the Marines were just about wiped out on Troy. Is that really the
situation?"

De Castro held a steady look on Gresser for several seconds, betraying nothing, before saying, "That's about the situation as I first heard it."

Gresser raised an eyebrow. "As you *first* heard it?"

"As you first heard what?" said another voice.

The two turned toward the door and saw Army Chief of Staff General John C. Robinson entering the War Room.

"Mr. Gresser was just trying to get a step up on everybody, that's all," de Castro said blandly. "Don't worry, he probably doesn't know anything that you don't. At least if he does he didn't get it from me."

Gresser blushed.

Robinson moved to the top of the table and took the seat at the left hand of the head chair, opposite where the Chairman would sit. "I hope somebody has a step up. All I've heard is we ran into a shitstorm on Troy, and are in danger of becoming one of those ruins-planets like we've found a few times."

De Castro shook his head. "My analysis suggests it's not that bad. Not quite."

"Your analysis is why you're here, of course," said Commandant of the Marine Corps, General Ralph Talbot as he stepped into the room. He looked grim.

"Keep your seats," Hobson said, striding in directly behind Talbot. The Chairman of the Joint Chiefs, Fleet Admiral Ira Welborn, came in with the Secretary of War.

Hobson glanced around and snarled, "Where the hell's Madison?"

"I'm here, sir," Madison said, sounding out of breath. His face was flushed; he must have run to get to the meeting.

"Secure the door behind yourself," Hobson ordered. He took his seat at the head of the table while the CNO closed the door, completing the seal that blocked all signals, audible or electronic, from leaving the room.

"You've all read Avery's messages." It wasn't a question; he'd immediately have the resignation of any member of the Joint Chiefs who hadn't read it. "Comments."

"I'm still absorbing the loss of VII Corps," Robinson said. "Admiral Avery wasn't very clear on which ships were killed. We need to find out what elements are still combat capable." He shook his head sadly. "Lyman is a major loss to the Army."

Hobson grunted. "Next."

"I'm embarrassed," Madison said. "I had no idea Callighan was that incompetant."

"Explain yourself," Welborn snapped.

Madison started at being spoken to so sharply. "Why... why, what other excuse could there be for losing an entire ARG?" he sputtered.

"The ships of the ARG were unarmed, and Rear Admiral Callighan had no reason to believe his group would be attacked, much less the way it was."

"But—."

"Next," Hobson cut him off. Not for the first time, he thought he needed a new CNO.

Next was Talbot. "Lieutenant General Bauer is one of the best officers I have ever had the pleasure of knowing. Regardless of what Admiral Avery's message says, it stretches my credulity beyond the willing suspension of disbelief to think that his entire MCF could have been destroyed, or that it could be forced to evacuate the planet after only one action."

"Of course a Marine would think like that," Madison said, having regained his composure. He didn't notice the hard look Hobson directed at him.

"General de Castro, what is your analysis?" Hobson asked.

De Castro held up a finger. "We don't know how much of ARG 17 survived the attack." He raised a second finger. "Therefore, we do not know how much of VII Corps is still combat capable." A third finger went up. "Fully aside from the Marines' well-known propensity for self-aggrandizement, I agree with Commandant Talbot, the First MCF has not been defeated." He glanced at Talbot. "Which isn't to say they won't be. We need more intelligence. The question at this point is, how do we get it?" He looked at Madison. "My analysis suggests that the Navy send a surveillance ship to scan the system from the mouth of a wormhole."

"Sir," Gresser raised his hand. "Before we get to that, please excuse my ignorance, but just what does 'issue in doubt' mean?"

Hobson scowled. "It's a very polite way of saying that the most probable outcome of the situation in question is total failure."

Gresser nodded and looked at his hands folded on the table-top in front of him. That was what he thought, he'd just wanted confirmation. It was evident to him that President Mills thought so, too.

"If I may, sir?" Talbot said to SecWar. When Hobson signaled his consent, the Commandant said to the President's assistant, "A Navy officer sent that message early in a twentieth century war. The Marines believed they could have held out until a relief force arrived. But the message convinced higher command not to send relief. So the Marines and others—the ones who weren't killed when they surrendered—spent four years in prisoner of war camps."

"You sound like you think we should send more troops," Gresser said.

"I think the battle's not lost until the last infantryman is rooted out."

"Enough of the sidetalk," Hobson snapped. "Madison, I asked you a question. Can you send a stealth starship to gather intelligence from near the mouth of a wormhole in the Troy system?"

The CNO made a moue. "Yes we can," he said grudgingly. "But it will be risky. We don't know what kind of security the aliens have out there. They might have warships stationed at every possible wormhole entry point and ready to fire as soon as one opens."

"That's why it's called, 'going in harm's way,' Madison." Hobson shook his head disgustedly.

"Robinson, how is Second Army coming along?"

"The major command elements are in place and most of the component elements have been identified," the Army Chief of Staff said. "I'm not sure about the Marines." He looked a question at Talbot.

"Second and Third MCFs are on 96 hour standby for the personnel. Their major equipment can start moving to the elevators as soon as transportation is provided. Does that answer your question about Marine readiness, General?"

Robinson smiled faintly as he nodded at the Marine.

Hobson nodded, satisfied by Talbot's response. "Robinson, start putting the component elements of Second Army on standby. Madison, begin assembling naval transportation. Welborn, I'll leave arranging the civilian auxillary to you. De Castro, coordinate with

Madison on your intelligence needs. Unless somebody else has something important, that's it for this meeting."

Nobody else had anything, so they all stood to leave. Hobson was the last out. He turned toward his office, and looked curiously at a man running toward him.

"Sir," Joseph Gion, Hobson's Chief of Staff called out as he hustled along the corridor, "I think you'll want to call everybody back."

"What? Why?" Hobson asked, startled. "All of you," he called to the Chiefs of Staff, "wait one!" He looked at Gion. "What do you have?" he asked and snatched the flimsy Gion held out to him. He quickly scanned it, asked, "When did this come in?" and ordered the Joint Chiefs back into the War Room when told the message had arrived only ten minutes earlier.

Closed back in the War Room, Hobson held the flimsy out. "The Commandant was right. The Marines have not been defeated on Troy. I'll get you all copies of this later, but right now I'll read the most germane sentences. 'Elements of First MCF have twice encountered the alien invaders and decisively defeated them on each occasion.'

"That's one item, the other is a request; he wants 30,000 shot-guns and a month's combat load of ammunition for them, and canister for his artillery. He also requests two thousand additional Marines, including a Whiskey Company for each of the regiments in the MCF along with enough additional officers of appropriate ranks to staff a battalion."

"What's a Whiskey Company?" Madison asked.

Hobson nodded at Talbot to answer.

"It's a company-size unit outside the normal compliment of a battalion or regiment, used specifically as either a reserve or be doled out piecemeal to companies as replacements for casualties."

The Round Room, the Prairie Palace, Omaha,
Douglas County, Federal Zone, NAU

"What the hell's the matter with those people?" President Mills roared. "Don't they talk to each other?" He had just read Bauer's message, which thoroughly contradicted the message from Avery, which he'd read scant hours earlier.

"Evidently not in this instance," Hobson said calmly.

"What next?" Mills demanded. "Is someone else going to send a message saying that A R—, A R..., whatever the hell it was called, is fine and landed that Army force?"

"No, sir, I don't believe we will get any such message. I believe Admiral Avery was right when he said ARG 17 was severely injured. Possibly even as nearly destroyed as he said. What's next, sir, is the Joint Chiefs have begun mounting a larger force to retake Troy. The Navy is shortly going to request permission to commandeer a large segment of civilian interstellar shipping to augment its own fleet."

"The Navy doesn't have enough shipping of its own?" Mills asked, astounded.

"We've never had this large a force to send at one time."

Mills rapidly looked side to side, twisting from his shoulders, as though seeking something he knew wasn't there. "All right," he finally said, "what do you suggest?"

"Let me give the Chiefs the go-ahead."

"What about Congress?"

Hobson shrugged. "What about Congress? How did the honorables react when you told them about Troy and our response in the first place?"

"They'd already voted me war powers," Mills said softly, almost a murmur.

"There you are. Congress abdicated its war waging responsibility. They gave it to you, Mr. President. Congress can't do anything, not without revoking the war powers. I imagine that would be a lengthy process."

Mills studied Hobson from under lowered brows. "Do you think we'll succeed if we take the next step?"

"Bauer seems confident. And Talbot has the highest confidence in him. The rest of the Chiefs also have confidence in the Marines, at least in their ability to hold out until Second Army reaches them."

Someone had once told Mills that a mark of a great leader was to make snap decisions based on incomplete information. He had tried to follow that dictum during a long and successful political career. So far it had worked well for him.

"Do it," he said. "Send that army to relieve the Marines."

A Wormhole, Troy Space

A non-human fleet began disgorging.

DAVID SHERMAN IS THE AUTHOR OR CO-AUTHOR OF SOME THREE DOZEN BOOKS, MOST of which are about Marines in combat.

He has written about US Marines in Vietnam (the Night Fighters series and three other novels), and the DemonTech series about Marines in a fantasy world. The 18th Race trilogy is military science fiction.

Other than military, he wrote a non-conventional vampire novel, *The Hunt,* and a mystery, *Dead Man's Chest*. He has also released a collection of short fiction and non-fiction from early in his writing career, *Sherman's Shorts; the Beginnings*.

With Dan Cragg he wrote the popular *Starfist* series and its spin off series, *Starfist: Force Recon*—all about Marines in the Twenty-fifth Century.; and a Star Wars novel, *Jedi Trial*.

His books have been translated into Czech, Polish, German, and Japanese.

"Chitter Chitter Bang Bang" is set in the world of *Starfist: Double Jeopardy*.

He lives in sunny South Florida, where he doesn't have to worry about hypothermia or snow-shoveling-induced heart attacks. He invites readers to visit his website, www.novelier.com.